The 1940's Radio Hour

A Musical by Walton Jones

Based on an idea by Walton Jones and Carol Lees as originaly presented by The Ensemble Company and Yale Repertory Theatre and further developed by Arena Stage in Washington, D.C. Broadway production presented by Jujamcyn Productions, Joseph P. Harris, Ira Bernstein and Roger Berlind.

A SAMUEL FRENCH ACTING EDITION

SAMUEL FRENCH

FOUNDED 1830

New York Hollywood London Toronto

SAMUELFRENCH.COM

OPENING NIGHT, OCTOBER 7, 1979

ST. JAMES THEATRE

OPERATED BY JUJAMCYN THEATRES
RICHARD G. WOLFF, PRESIDENT

JUJAMCYN PRODUCTIONS, JOSEPH P. HARRIS, IRA BERNSTEIN AND ROGER BERLIND

present

Written by
WALTON JONES

The Company

**KATHY ANDRINI, DEE DEE BRIDGEWATER, JOHN DOOLITTLE,
ARNY FREEMAN, MERWIN GOLDSMITH, JOE GRIFASI,
JACK HALLETT, MARY CLEERE HARAN, STEPHEN JAMES,
JEFF KELLER, JOHN SLOMAN, JOSEF SOMMER, CRISSY WILZAK**

Scenic Design by	*Lighting Design by*	*Costume Design by*	*Sound Design by*
DAVID GROPMAN	THARON MUSSER	WILLIAM IVEY LONG	OTTS MUNDERLOH

Orchestrations by	*Vocal Arrangements by*	*General Manager*	*Production Stage Manager*
GARY S. FAGIN	PAUL SCHIERHORN	FRANK SCARDINO	ED ALDRIDGE

Furs by MICHAEL FORREST

Musical Supervision and Direction by
STANLEY LEBOWSKY

Musical Numbers Staged by
THOMMIE WALSH

Directed by
WALTON JONES

Based on an idea by Walton Jones and Carol Lees, as originally presented by The Ensemble Company and Yale Repertory
Theatre in New Haven and further developed and presented by The Arena Stage in Washington, D.C.

Poster art by Paul de Pass/ATD

The Producers and Theatre Management are Members
of The League of New York Theatres and Producers, Inc.

Clifton A. Feddington and Saul Lebowitz

present

The Mutual Manhattan

V A R I E T Y   C A V A L C A D E

in a live broadcast from the Hotel Astor's Algonquin Room, Broadway
between 44th and 45th Streets New York City

December 21, 1942

with
GINGER BROOKS,
GENEVA LEE BROWNE, ANN COLLIER,
B.J. GIBSON and CONNIE MILLER,
RAY OWEN, NEAL TILDEN

and
JOHNNY CANTONE

featuring
THE ZOOT DOUBLEMAN ORCHESTRA
Zoot Doubleman, Keyboards

Phil Bentley, Bass

Custis Lee Jones, Guitar

Neeley "Flap" Kovacs, Drums

Reeds
Toots Schoenfeld
Charlie "Kid Lips" Snyder
Bonnie Cavanaugh
Ned "Woof" Bennett
Fess "Snookie" Davenport
Gus Bracken

Trombones	Trumpets
Fritz Canigliaro	Pieface Minelli
Bob "Bobo" Lewis	Moe "Lockjaw" Ambrose
Scoops Millikin	Buzz Cranshaw
	Biff Baker

Musical Direction, Zoot Doubleman
Vocal Arrangements, Niles Doubleman
Orchestrations, Sidney Neumark
Musical Staging and Stage Management, Lou Cohn
Doorman for the Algonquin Room, Mr. Arthur Bailey
Technician, Stanley Gallagher

CAST

(in order of appearance)

Pops Bailey .... ARNY FREEMAN
Stanley .... JOHN SLOMAN
Clifton A. Feddington .... JOSEF SOMMER
Zoot Doubleman .... STANLEY LEBOWSKY
Wally Fergusson .... JACK HALLETT
Lou Cohn .... MERWIN GOLDSMITH
Johnny Cantone .... JEFF KELLER
Ginger Brooks .... CRISSY WILZAK
Connie Miller .... KATHY ANDRINI
B. J. Gibson .... STEPHEN JAMES
Neal Tilden .... JOE GRIFASI
Ann Collier .... MARY-CLEERE HARAN
Geneva Lee Browne .... DEE DEE BRIDGEWATER
Biff Baker .... JOHN DOOLITTLE

THE ORCHESTRA

Zoot Doubleman — STANLEY LEBOWSKY; Neeley "Flap" Kovacs —
MAURICE MARK; Bonnie Cavanaugh — JANE IRA BLOOM; Custis Jones —
BILLY BUTLER; Gus Bracken — RAY SHANFELD; Scoops Millikan
— DENNIS ELLIOTT; Moe "Lockjaw" Ambrose — JOSH EDWARDS; Biff
Baker — JOHN DOOLITTLE; Fritz Canigliaro — JOE PETRIZZO; Charlie
"Kid Lips" Snyder — DENNIS ANDERSON; Ned "Woof" Bennett — J. D.
PARRAN; Totts Schoenfeld — MEL RODNON; Fess "Snookie" Davenport —
RICK CENTALONZA; Bob "Bobo" Lewis — JON GOLDMAN; Buzz Cran-
shaw — RON TOOLEY; — Phil Bentley — BRUCE SAMUELS; Pieface
Minelli—LLOYD MICHELS.

CAST:
8-10 men (two are also orchestra members)
2-4 women

ORCHESTRA:
5-17 pieces

The size of the cast may be reduced by cutting the characters of GENEVA and STANLEY, by combining the characters of NEAL and WALLY into WALLY, and/or by combining the characters of GINGER and CONNIE into GINGER. If the character of GENEVA is cut, cut "ROSE OF THE RIO GRANDE" from the show and re-assign "I GOT IT BAD AND THAT AIN'T GOOD" to the character of ANN. When cuts or combinations are made, adapt and cut the dialogue as necessary.

The orchestra has been scored for seventeen pieces, however the orchestration can be adapted to thirteen pieces, nine pieces, seven pieces, or rhythm and horn. (In the original production of THE 1940's RADIO HOUR, the ZOOT DOUBLEMAN ORCHESTRA was just a piano)

The vintage microphones referred to in the script are the RCA 44BX, the RCA 77D, the RCA 74, and the Westinghouse "eight ball" microphone. These, and other period microphones may be purchased from such reconditioning houses as Boynton Studios, Melody Pines Farm, Morris, New York 13808; (607) 263-5695. Period magazines, for research or for use as props, can be purchased from Mr. Johnny Roberts, Prince Back Issues, 750 Ninth Avenue, New York, New York 10036; (212) 581-6740.

This production is played without an intermission.

The 1940's Radio Hour

The seedy studios of WOV, a 5,000-watt local New York City radio station, about an hour before a Monday night broadcast of a weekly variety show, "The Mutual Manhattan Variety Cavalcade," December 21, 1942.

The set can be as simple as a bandstand and some chairs, or as elaborate in its tawdriness as production will allow. The tawdrier the better. If you were going to go all the way, you might want something like this:

Right, a greenroom. A desk, some chairs and stools, mailboxes, call board, magazines on a table, a time clock, a coffee urn above which are personalized mugs on pegs in the wall, a pay phone on the wall Downstage of the door to the outside on which is stenciled "Shubert Alley Exit." A Coke machine with a hand-written "Out of Order" sign taped over the coin slot, a dirty linoleum floor. In the corner, a mop and bucket. On the shelf above the desk and below the mailboxes which are decorated with a string of Christmas cards, is a radio. Outside, a blizzard and neon lights, occasionally passing traffic, maybe the tease of a fire escape and an outside light with "Stage" written on its globe. A room Upstage of the greenroom. An anteroom where there are coat-racks, a chair or two, a full-length mirror, tables and magazines, a calendar on the wall, and a door that leads to the control room above. And a bay window that faces Shubert Alley and Forty-Fifth Street, through which you can see, barely through the snow, the neon light of the Piccadilly Drug Store across the street.

Left, upholstered doors which lead to a hallway which leads to the dressing rooms, other studios and the "Broadway Exit" of the building. Signs in the hall point directions to "Studio A," "Studio B," and "1402," as well as to the Broadway exit. Up Left, another door, the pebbleglass top-half of which reads, "Feddington Productions. Private."

In the studio, "Studio B," dark now except for the ghost light, is a music-standed bandstand, on risers about four feet off the floor which, like the greenroom, is lineoleum; a covered ebony baby-grand piano; shrouded microphones which line the front of the stage and hang from booms in the orchestra. Upstage and slightly above the bandstand is the control booth. The dark glass front of the booth keeps us from seeing too much, but inside there are dials and lights and a clock with a sweep second hand. Left, near the doors to the other studios, a sound effects booth with every conceivable sound effect crowded onto a four-by-six table.

When the door to "Feddington Productions" is open, you can see the corner of CLIFTON'S *desk and his telephone, the side of his typewriter, stacks of papers, a filing cabinet—like three offices piled into one. To the outside of that door, on the studio wall, many light dimmers and switches which supposedly control the dozens of instruments hanging from the ceiling. Next to the dimmers, tie-offs for the "flies." On the ceiling in the center, an enormous lighting fixture: a chandelier which has several concentric circles which can individually light up.*

In the greenroom, on top of the Coke machine, a Christmas tree, small and tacky, decorated with one pathetic string of lights; eyeball scoops and a utility light in a mesh cage.

On the back wall of the studio and in the control booth are the studio clocks. As the broadcast is actually more than an hour, the clocks will have to be slowed down or stopped occasionally during the broadcast. Ideally, they should also be able to run about three times as fast as normal during the "pre-show" so that what is actually only about eighteen minutes long could represent the whole hour before the broadcast.

This studio is the home of a group of working-class entertainers—slightly disreputable and decidedly second-rate in all their attempts. The set looks worn-out. Before the broadcast, so do they. They have all come from second jobs: ANN *from her job as a secretary somewhere,* GINGER *from a restaurant where she is a waitress,* B.J. *from New Haven where he goes to school,* CONNIE *from her elevator operator job in the Hotel Astor,* NEAL *is a cab driver, etc.*

"Pops" Bailey *is the stage doorman. Over 60. The traditionally wizened, crotchety, miserable, crusty, foul-tempered stage door keeper who makes book on the company phone and reads hidden copies of "Show Girl." Listens to the races and other shows on his radio during the broadcast. Quits every night. Always mopping up—actually just moving the dirt around with a mop that should have been condemned years ago. Has been fixing the Coke machine for six months. It works for him, or anyone who knows the secret kick. Plays cards with* Lou, *the stage manager. Concerned with keeping the Life magazines in order so he can tell who's winning the War. He moves slowly. Stands still a lot. Makes the easy marks: the eager* B.J., *the know-it-all* Neal *and* Wally, *the delivery boy. Admires* Johnny Cantone, *but of all of them, is really fond of only* Ann. *Always ready to start an argument or start into a conversation he's not a part of. Has a muttered, mumbled gripe that seems to run under the whole show. Was in World War I. Has a son in the Pacific. Chomps on a frequently unlit cigar and hardly ever calls anyone but* Lou *by their real names, but by "Pal," "Buster," "Charlie," and "Bub."*

Lou Cohn *is busy keeping the true stage manager's tradition by being the entrepreneur's entrepreneur. About forty. Big shot. Always trying to impress* Ginger, *the waitress whose job here* Lou *is responsible for. Keeps four or five conversations going at once, and all of them straight. Chubby and balding. Wears a hat because he's sensitive about his hairline. The surrogate boss during rehearsals which he conducts. Choreographs the numbers. Plays rehearsal piano like a Nazi. Echoes everything* Clifton *says. Officious and obnoxious sometimes. Hardass about the seriousness of his job. Unlike anyone else,* Lou *has no ambitions to be anything else but stage manager. He is perfectly content with a job that has plenty of authority and no responsibility. Cues the audience,* Clifton, *the band, the performers, performs the sound effects, runs the lights and controls all of the stage "effects." Takes his cues from a headset he wears over his hat.*

Clifton A. Feddington *is the band leader, announcer, general manager, head-of-everything at WOV. Co-produces with* Saul Lebowitz, *who we don't see but whose phone calls we sometimes hear about. Has a dark, cluttered office which we only see glimpses of during the show. Corporate offices at 1648 Broadway, above the deli. Has a deaf secretary. And ulcers. We see him in various states of hysteria; carrying contracts, letters, running his hand through his hair. Always has problems. Always with his Bromo. A bigger entrepreneur than* LOU. *Has more corporate tax dodges than Westinghouse. But his luck's not so great. Founded "Clifton Records: the signature series" just in time for the 1942 record industry strike. Sells commercial time on the Calvacade real cheap to attract lots of listeners since the number of sponsors means the show must be popular. He, and everyone associated with this station, treat this and every broadcast as if the world's listening. And every night is an audition for a network slot since who knows who may be listening in? A real cheapskate. Very genuine and vulnerable. A Jimmy Stewart with a mic style like a young Bob Hope. Not too effective as a Warner Baxter type but he tries to be. Even has trouble hyping the audience during ads. But that's his charm. He and the others survive every catastrophe, every foul-up, every goof-up, every goof-off. Lives a paper chase from his office to the greenroom and back and forth and back and forth. Wears a William Powell moustache. Working at WOV since 1936 when he got the job from* JOHNNY CANTONE'S, *uncle, Salvatore D'Angelis.*

NEAL TILDEN *is the comic who drives a cab. Son of the wealthy Tildens of Gramercy Park. Got cut-out of the will because he was "a bum in show business." Lives with his mother. Wants to do it all: sing, dance, comedy, act, lead the band, choreograph.* CLIFTON *won't even give him a ballad. Been at the station since the beginning. Came in with* ANN COLLIER *and* JOHNNY CANTONE *when things were just starting. Really tight. Keeps his money in a teeny clip purse. Still hoping for the "featured vocalist" slot if* JOHNNY *ever leaves. Has seniority (he thinks). The resident crybaby. A real whiner. Always sneaking around doing things he's not supposed to be doing. Always putting everybody else down—especially* CANTONE *who he admires a lot. Gets called into* CLIFTON'S *office pretty regularly for early-morning chew-outs. Carries a pipe for the "right look." Horses around a lot during the broadcasts. Has trick pants that drop during his comedy shtick to help get laughs. Pants that unfortunately continue to fall at inappropriate times during the broadcast. Treats* WALLY *like* CANTONE *treats him. Always has advice and "big news" for* WALLY. *Wants to be important. Would like to be in love with* ANN, *but doesn't even try. At the bottom line, a very lonely guy who's the clown. (This character may be combined with* WALLY. *Adapt and cut dialogue as necessary.)*

ANN COLLIER, *the old standard in* CLIFTON'S *Cavalcade: she's been there since it started in 1936. She works during the day as a secretary for a large corporation—a private secretary for the boss. Has been married once. "Dating"* JOHNNY CANTONE *at the moment. Must sound like the "big band vocalists" of the period: has a voice like Peggy Lee, Ginny Simms, Dinah Shore, Doris Day, Helen Forrest, all rolled into one. A gorgeous redhead. Dances in the "Blue Moon" number a kind of reverse Astaire/Rogers routine: she does all the dancing while* NEAL *stands still. Sings the song to the boys overseas. Gets offers all the time but claims she is perfectly happy where she is.*

GENEVA LEE BROWNE *is a beautiful, high-class, black singer from Kansas City where she played the Chesterfield Club with her own group, the Chocolate Drops. Started in New York at fifteen in the Hot Chocolates Revue at the Cotton Club. Is a songwriter and plays the piano. Sings one song like Ella Fitzgerald with lots of scat and sass, the other song is simple and bluesy. Conducts the band during her numbers. Wears a gardenia in her hair. Comes in with members of her band: a trombonist, a bassist, a reed and a couple of others—all black—who play in* ZOOT'S *band now and before and after hours at various jazz clubs on Fifty-Second Street. Her second job is singing. And her third job. And her fourth job. She is always performing and always dressed to kill. A musician. Plays piano, but sings like it's an instrument too. Sassy, brassy and loud with a Pearl Bailey. (Note: This character can be cut. Adapt and cut dialogue as necessary.)*

BIFF BAKER *started with* ZOOT *when the band was only a six-piece combo in 1936 on WOV. From Chicago. Plays trumpet or saxophone in the band. Like Beneke. Carries his horn in a wrinkled brown bag. Has been playing with Glenn Miller for the last few months and the Cavalcade every week off and on since 1936 and, most recently, while in training at Ft. Bragg, New Jersey. This is* BIFF's *last show. Tomorrow he goes overseas in a fighter squadron. Baby-faced. Mid-twenties. Enters in uniform. Has a girlfriend in Park Ridge, Illinois that he's been dating since high school. Sings and plays in the band.*

CONNIE MILLER *is the seventeen-year-old bobbysoxer from Ogden, Utah. Born about ten years too late: would have been a great Berkley girl. Always in love. "Seriously dating"* B.J. GIBSON. *Very young. Enthusiastic. Taps and jitterbugs. Swoons for* CANTONE. *Only been with the Cavalcade since the fall. Has a little Judy Garland in her. Sings like Marian Hutton. Drinks twelve Cokes during the show and lines the bottles up under her chair. Has a pushy mother who is trying to get her into show business. Hangs with* GINGER, *who acts as kind of a big sister to her. An elevator operator at the Astor Hotel during the day. (This character may be combined with the character of* GINGER. *Adapt and cut dialogue as necessary.)*

JOHNNY CANTONE *is the featured vocalist with the Cavalcade, who is on Sinatra's bandwagon. He and hundreds of other guys. From Brooklyn. Ex-welterweight boxer. Rough guy. Always pinching* NEAL's *cheek and slapping him. Somewhere between a late-forties to late-fifties Sinatra sound. Has got the public sass of the latter. Class. Wears a diamond pinky ring that he "plays" in the lights during his numbers. Voice like velvet. Drinks during the show. And sometimes during his numbers. Which galls* CLIFTON *but* JOHNNY's *uncle got* CLIFTON *the job, so what can you do? Smarmy and greasy but as much of a punk as he is, he is also a sweet, vulnerable, sad little kid who plays a tough guy to protect himself. Gets pretty sloshed during the show. Not a particularly funny sloshed either. Married. Wears a wedding band. But his wife, Angel, left him years ago. Been with* CLIFTON *since the beginning. Now in his thirties. Pays bobbysoxers to scream for him at the stage door. Dating* ANN *at the moment. Or, as* GINGER *says, "They share the same bar." Interested in* CONNIE *most obviously but isn't too choosey. He'd go with anything that would hold still long enough. All the flirting, successful or not, gives great boosts to his ego. Doesn't get along with* GINGER. *Waves to the audience before and after numbers. Throws flowers to them. Gets away with all the dramatics he sings with because he is good. So good that the waste is even more painful to watch.*

GINGER BROOKS *is the bubble-headed waitress-turned-star discovery of* LOU'S *who found her in a restaurant where she still works and conned* CLIFTON *into signing her on. Caricatured but the parody is her own. Leads with her lower lip like Betty Boop. Pinup, Betty Grable look. She rehearses in a slip. Chews gum but takes it out of her mouth and holds it while she's performing. When she's sitting and her legs are crossed, and she's not adjusting the seams in her stockings, she wiggles her foot back and forth. Always moving. Has the biggest Keane blue eyes in history. Has a cab driver boyfriend named Bruno. Gets away with murder. Acts as* CONNIE'S *big sister. Speaks with a Gracie Allen vacancy. Her makeup is as important as the War. And is always "thick and perfect." (This character may be combined with* CONNIE. *Adapt and cut dialogue as necessary.)*

B.J. GIBSON *is the third of the* GIBSON *brothers to work for* CLIFTON. *Tall, preppy, about twenty; a student at Yale who commutes to the weekend rehearsals and Monday night performances. Dating* CONNIE. *Taps and jitterbugs. Really aggressive about his career. Always wants to know how he did and elicits praise from people whose opinions he respects. Worships* CANTONE *but keeps it a secret. Picks up tips everywhere—especially from* CANTONE. *Good-looking. Squeaky-clean, Dick Powell look.*

WALLY FERGUSSON *is the poodle-eyed young hopeful from Altoona, Pennsylvania who came to New York to work for his uncle at the drugstore and hopefully get his big break into show business. We never see his* UNCLE DOMINIC, *but we hear his phone calls. In love with him the minute you see him. Attends every rehearsal and performance when they'll let him. Always practicing everyone else's routines in case they ever need him.* POPS' *albatross. Makes deliveries during the show but inevitably leaves most of them in the studio while he hangs around. Piles of bags by the end of the show. Works in the Piccadilly Drug Store on Forty-Fifth street. These folks are the biggest stars in the world to him, especially* CANTONE. *Goes on tonight for Ray Owen and tries real hard but screws up everything he's a part of. (This character may be combined with* NEAL. *Adapt and cut dialogue as necessary.)*

ZOOT DOUBLEMAN *is the bandleader and plays the piano in "The most versatile band in the land." More at home with the musicians and shares jokes with them. About fifty and tired.*

STANLEY *is about twenty. Lugs cable and runs around a lot and otherwise lives in the control booth. Drinks coffee and eats constantly. Has a thing for* GINGER *whose numbers he watches a little more animatedly. Not too bright. Punches in like* POPS *and* LOU. *(Note: This character may be cut. Adapt and cut dialogue as necessary.)*

We are watching the last-minute preparations of this clutch of characters as they ready themselves for this live broadcast from New York City that they have been rehearsing for all week.

These are working-class performers. They wear street clothes. No furs. Nothing fancy. Except for CANTONE, *they probably make very little money outside of this job and certainly very little here. Every effort should be made to keep them looking like* real *people—the people whose pictures appeared in all of those Life Magazines from the period. Just ordinary folks with varying degrees of ambition and self-imposed parody. And there can be nothing glitsy about the broadcast. Their every attempt at being "big time" with production values must prove that the "big time" is not within their reach.*

When the real audience is seated in the theatre, activity Onstage has already begun. POPS' *radio is playing in the house as well so that even if they wanted to, the audience would not be able to hear what is being said. The clock Onstage says that it is about 7:30 P.M. and, if possible, runs fast so that the eighteen minute or so pre-show could represent a whole hour of pre-broadcast activity. The audience is given two programs: one real and one "fake." The "fake" program is the program of the Mutual Manhattan Variety Cavalcade and contains bios of the performers and their forties glamour photographs if possible. These bios contain more clues about these people and their lives in the forties. The back of that program might be an advertisement from one of the period sponsors, in period form. Telephone company, Coca Cola. All effort to preserve the illusion that this is really taking place. The PERFORMERS don't actually "see" the audience until "places" are called by* Lou *just before the broadcast. (Note: the "copy" for the fake program follows this script.)*

The clocks Onstage run at regular speed during the half-hour before the house lights fade. They read 7:30. The night light is Onstage. POPS *sits at his desk. He goes into his drawer. Makes a phone call. Takes out his mug and cleans it with a soiled hanky from his trousers pocket. He takes a call on the pay phone and writes something down on the wall. He tunes his radio. The music is playing in the house too. A Will Bradley broadcast from the Astor Roof. He looks up.* STAN *stands Center, looking out into the "empty house," sipping coffee from a cardboard container. He wears a white shirt, baggy pants and suspenders. A pile of cable at his feet.* POPS *cleans his cup. The phone rings. The pay phone.* POPS *answers it as* STAN *finishes his coffee and heads off into the anteroom.* POPS *reads from his piece of paper and then writes something on the wall next to the phone, shielding it from* STAN *who is passing him but doesn't care.* STAN *picks up the cable and* POPS *watches him leave and* CLIFTON *comes in from the hallway carrying music and talking to* ZOOT. *He goes into his office with* ZOOT *and* POPS *cleans his cup with a soiled hanky from his trouser pocket.*

WALLY *enters with some deliveries.* POPS *throws him out.* CLIFTON *comes back out of his office with papers and tousled hair. Looks concerned. He goes into the hallway and* ZOOT *stops off at the piano for a second then follows.* CLIFTON *mutters hello to* STAN *as he goes by.* STAN *doesn't answer but keeps plugging along at what he's doing.* STAN *is a tinkerer. He always has something to do because he takes so long to do things and he always does them at the same time.* POPS *checks that the coast is clear and takes out his copy of "Show Girl" to read but the phone rings before he can read it. It's for* CLIFTON, *who* POPS *starts off to get, but* CLIFTON'S *already on his way back in with* ZOOT, *arguing about the length of an arrangement they're planning for a future show.* CLIFTON *gets the message, and takes it at* POPS' *desk phone.* POPS *is uncomfortable with* CLIFTON *in his space.* CLIFTON *goes into his office to take the call.* POPS *listens in.* CLIFTON *catches him.* ZOOT *is sketching out some new arrangement leaning on the piano.* POPS *pours his coffee real meticulously. Sugar. Goes outside to get the cream he's left on the stoop. Puts his sweater up over his head.*

WALLY *re-enters without seeing* POPS *and inadvertently shuts the door, locking* POPS *out.* POPS *appears at the window and knocks. Yells as he knocks a second time which cannot be heard at all.* WALLY *attempts to figure out what* POPS *is saying rather than letting him in.* ZOOT *lets him back in. He throws* WALLY *out again but* WALLY *distracts him and sneaks in anyway.* POPS *continues the ritual with the coffee.* CLIFTON *comes through and is looking for something on and in* POPS' *desk. After* CLIFTON *leaves,* POPS *re-lights his cigar stump and settles back with his coffee to read "Show Girl" magazine.*

WALLY *is in the studio dipping the mic seductively like a singer.*

STAN *orders something from him. He writes it all down on his pad. The pay phone rings.* POPS *gets it, but it's for* WALLY, *who dashes back into the snow for more deliveries.* POPS *looks at the floor and shakes his head. He gets the mop and mops it up. He complains to himself. A running mutter.* LOU *comes in and punches in.* POPS *complains about the mess and* LOU *kicks his shoes off while the door is open.* WALLY *comes back in.* POPS *puts his collar up because it's so cold and shouts at someone to close the door. More mess.* WALLY *asks* LOU *about Ray Owen.* LOU *says no news yet.* POPS *gives up with the mopping. Telephone rings. Pay phone. For* WALLY *again although* POPS *gets it.* POPS *shows* WALLY *the way out.* POPS *somehow gets locked out again.* STAN *is bringing on a step ladder. Then* STAN *brings in the instrument and cable with a half a sandwich in his mouth.* LOU *lets* POPS *back inside and shows* POPS *how to lock it open.*

This kind of activity continues until the show is ready to begin. This silent, or at least inaudible activity is the kind of activity which accompanies the broadcast: behind-the-scenes playing out of life. At the cue to begin the show, maybe a telephone call to POPS, POPS *eventually finds himself alone Onstage and sees that the Christmas tree lights are not lit. After testing whether or not they are plugged in (they are), he sees the culprit light and screws it in more tightly and the whole string lights up.* CLIFTON *comes back in grumbling about something and slams his door.* POPS *watches.* LOU *watches. From the anteroom where he has taken his coat.* HOUSE LIGHTS ARE FADING AND THE RADIO FADES INTO THE PRACTICAL ONSTAGE. CANTONE *comes in from the hallway with a drink and a cigarette which he drops at the piano. Picks up his coat and starts putting it on.* POPS *is shuffling the cards loudly. The pay phone rings and* POPS *answers it and writes something on the wall. It is 8:00.*

This next section should run about twenty minutes. It should be played quickly and with much overlapping of lines. Some scenes might even be played simultaneously. There is almost always a bustle Onstage; a bustle which grows in intensity as the broadcast time approaches. Once they have entered, the CHARACTERS are very "present"—whether they have lines or not.

JOHNNY. (*As he is leaving.*) Don't wait up for me.

(LOU *comes out of the anteroom, sees the coast is clear. No* CLIFTON *to see him not working.* POPS *has finished dealing and is studying his hand like it's a national secret. He arranges his cards as* LOU *picks his cup off the wall and blows the dust out of it and begins to fill it with* POPS' *coffee.* POPS *is drinking his own cup, enjoying it a lot, as* LOU *has filled it partway and has cocked it to one side looking into it like something is moving in it. He looks at* POPS, *takes the lid off the urn and pours it back in and blesses himself. He goes to the Coke machine and sees the out of order sign.*)

LOU. I thought you were gonna fix this.

POPS. It works perfectly. You've just got to know how to handle it.

(LOU *realizes the routine he has to do to get the Coke out and proceeds to kick the machine.* POPS *leaps to his feet.* LOU *freezes.*)

Hey!

(POPS *puts down his cards and walks over to the Coke machine.* LOU *steps aside for the master.* POPS *performs the miracle and the Coke comes.* LOU *opens it and opens a Hostess Cupcake.*)

Why don't you have some coffee, I just made some fresh.

Lou. Don't do me any favors.

(*Pay phone rings.* Pops *answers it.*)

Pops. Yeah? I got a tip on Blond Boy in the second. A deuce? You got it. (Pops *writes the bet on the wall. Sitting down to the game. Suavely.*) Okay.

Lou. Where's Clifton?

Pops. (*Gesturing.*) In his office.

Lou. One hand Pops.

Pops. (*Pretty cocky.*) That's all it takes.

(Lou *picks up his hand and arranges his cards quickly and efficiently, draining the Coke and finishing the cupcake as he does so.* Stan *comes in with another instrument and climbs the ladder to put it in.* Pops *panicked. "Chicken Little".*)

Hey Buster! What're you doing with that? What're you doing with that? Hey Pal, I'm talking to you. Did anybody tell you you could do that?

(Pops *is standing. Still holding his cards.* Lou *is playing and* Stan *keeps working.*)

Who told you you could do that? Lou. Hey Lou. The kid is fooling with the lights. What're you doing with that? Who told you you could do that? Lou, he's mucking with the lights. Hey come down from there. Lou. Hey Lou.

(Stan *finishes and goes back into the booth to try the lights.*)

Lou. Thanks, Stanley.

Stan. Sure, Mr. Cohn. (*Exits to control room.*)

Pops. (*Trying to be boss.*) Yeah. Thanks, Stanley. Good thinking, Lou. I was gonna fix that light.

Lou. (*Matter-of-factly putting down cards in bunches.*) Boom boom boom.

Pops. What happened?

Lou. I won.

Pops. Already?

(Lou *makes a note of the winning in his notebook.* Pops *studies the disaster on the desk without touching any of the evidence. The desk phone rings. Still in shock.*)

WOV, New York City, may I help you? Just a moment. (*Screams.*) Clifton, pick up the phone!

Clifton. (*Coming to his door. Wild-eyed.*) Use the intercom, Pops.

Pops. It doesn't work.

Clifton. Use it anyway.

Lou. Good evening, Mr. Feddington.

Clifton. Get to work, Lou.

Lou. Yes, Mr. Feddington.

(Pops *stops.* Clifton *slams the door He doesn't hang up the phone but listens in.* Clifton's *door opens.*)

Clifton. Can you hear okay, Pops?

(Pops *quickly puts the phone back on the receiver. The phone is tucked between* Clifton's *shoulder and his ear and he is still talking as he shuts the door. Into the phone.*)

No, it's just the doorman.

(*Goes back into his office.* Wally *comes in from the outside.*)

Pops. Nobody's here yet, Wally.

Wally. I know.

(*To* Stan *who's rounding the bend with* Lou's *headset.*)

Here's your coffee, sir.

Stan. Thanks, Wally.

Wally. No problem.

Lou. Get to work Stanley.

Stan. Yes, Mr. Cohn.

(Stan *gives* Wally *some money and* Wally *flips the coin around.*)

Wally. Thank *you*, sir.

Lou. It's your discard, Pops.

Pops. No it isn't.

Lou. Yes it is.

Pops. No it isn't.

Lou. Yes it is.

Pops. It is not.

Lou. Okay. (*Plays a card.*) Boom boom boom.

Pops. (*Looks at the disaster.*) It was my discard.

Lou. That's what I told you.

Pops. (*Surveys the disaster. To* Wally *who he realizes is looking too.*) Don't you have some deliveries to make?

Lou. Wally, be a nice kid and get me some hot chocolate.

Wally. (*Like he's placing an order.*) One hot chocolate. Hey Lou, you think Mr. Feddington might let me stay for the broadcast tonight?

Lou. No, and don't ask him.

Clifton. (*Exploding out of his office with a sheaf of papers.*) Where the hell is everybody, Lou?

Lou. (*Quickly.*) Good evening, Mr. Feddington, just

straightening up a little before I go to work. Wally, I think you'd better be moving along.

CLIFTON. Wally, bring me a coffee, will you?

LOU. Wally, bring Mr. Feddington a coffee. How would you like that coffee, sir?

CLIFTON. (*Hurrying around.*) Black.

LOU. Black, Wally, black.

WALLY. One black coffee.

POPS. I just made some coffee.

LOU. It's not dead yet.

(*Pay phone rings.* CLIFTON *is posting a notice on the call board.*)

POPS. (*Answering phone.*) Yeah? Go ahead. (*Writing.*) Yeah. (*Raising his voice.*) No no no. Hialeah, whaddiya think, they run in the snow? Alright. Bashful Daddy in the third to win. Five bucks. You got it, Bub.

CLIFTON. What was that?

POPS. (*Innocent.*) What was what?

CLIFTON. Are you making book on the phone?

POPS. (*Easily.*) No.

CLIFTON. Goddammit, Pops!

POPS. Oh, quit beefing.

CLIFTON. I've told you not to use our phones to place bets.

POPS. I'm not placing bets. I'm taking them.

(GINGER *and* CONNIE *enter from the outside.*)

GINGER. (*To* LOU.) Hi, punkin'.

LOU. Hi, Toots.

CONNIE. Hi, Pops.

POPS. Don't track up my nice clean floor. I was in here all morning.

LOU. Connie, call your mother.

CLIFTON. Lou, you better start calling Owen. Ginger, you're late.

LOU. Sure thing, Mr. Feddington. Ginger, you're late. (*He looks up the number.*)

POPS. Look at that. Goddamit, I quit, Lou.

LOU. You can't quit, Pops.

POPS. Just watch me! (POPS *is attempting to mop through the above with all of them in the way. The pay phone rings.*)

LOU. Hey Wally, how about that hot chocolate?

WALLY. Right, Lou.

LOU. And a coffee for Clifton.

WALLY. No problem.

POPS. (*He picks up the pay phone.*) Yeah. My Nephew Wally. In what race? Oh. (*Handing the phone to* WALLY.) It's your Uncle Dominic. Make it quick.

CONNIE. (*Taking off her coat.*) Did my mom sound upset?

WALLY. Hi, Uncle Dom.

LOU. She just wants you to check in.

WALLY. I'll make those deliveries in a minute. I promise. (*He hangs up.*)

POPS. Okay, smart guy.

LOU. (*To* POPS *who is holding a new hand.*) What's that?

POPS. Three out of four.

LOU. (*Holding the phone in one hand and the cards in the other.*) You asked for it. (*Yells.*) Stanley!

WALLY. Why are you calling Ray Owen?

STANLEY. Yes, Mr. Cohn?

LOU. (*Dialing phone.*) Stanley, look at the time. It's 8:20 and this place isn't even set up yet.

STAN. Sorry, Mr. Cohn.

LOU. (*Into the phone.*) Ray Owen, fourth floor.

STAN. I was testing that light I put up.

LOU. Test it later. Move the chairs. (*To* WALLY.) One of those for me? (LOU *takes a hot dog from one of* WALLY's *deliveries.*)

POPS. Hey, Lou, you got the club?

(LOU *plays a card.*)

WALLY. Why, you think he's not gonna show up tonight?

POPS. That's the spade.

LOU. (*Taking the card back. And plays another.*) Ray Owen, Ray Owen, what are you, deaf?

POPS. I knew you had it.

LOU. (*To* STANLEY.) Not those chairs, the chairs in the hall. (*Into the phone.*) Yeah? (*To* POPS.) You already discarded, Pops.

POPS. No I didn't.

LOU. Yes you did. (*Into the phone.*) Well, get him. I can't wait all night.

WALLY. I know those numbers, Lou.

POPS. Okay, Lou, I played the four.

LOU. (*To* POPS.) You can't play the four, whaddiya think that is. (*Into the phone.*) This is Lou Cohn down at the radio station.

WALLY. I've been at every rehearsal this week.

POPS. How could there be five fours?

Lou. (*To* Pops.) There aren't five fours. Two's are wild. Your four doesn't mean spit. (*Into the phone.*) Yeah, when he gets out of the tub, you tell that red nose to call me right away and don't even stop to get a towel. (*Hangs up.*)

Pops. If I can't play the four, what can I play?

Wally. I can do it, Lou. I practice at home even. Maybe not the song, but I know the backup stuff.

Lou. (*To* Wally.) Don't be ridiculous. (*To* Pops.) Play the seven.

Pops. Good idea.

Lou. (*Putting his cards down.*) Boom boom boom.

Pops. What happened?

Lou. You shouldn't listen to me.

(*The radio on* Pops's *desk is still playing.* Ginger *and* Connie *come back into the greenroom without their coats.* Ginger *checks her mail.* Wally *wanders around the studio.* Stanley *has stopped setting up the chairs.* Lou *makes a note of his winning.* Connie *picks up* Pops' *desk phone to use it.*)

Pops. Hey, Sister, what's wrong with the pay phone?

Connie. I haven't got a nickel.

Pops. So borrow one.

(Connie *puts the receiver down and the phone rings.* Pops *looks at her like "I told you so" and answers the phone. Into phone. At first cheerfully.*)

WOV New York City, may I help you? The Mutual Manhattan Variety Cavalcade. Of course it's a variety show! Didn't I just say that, you dummy? Nine o'clock! (*He slams down the phone. To* Lou *who is looking at him.*) Public relations.

(Neal *enters from the alley, leaving the door open.*)

Neal. (*Like the mad Russian.*) How do you do! (*A snowball flies in, hitting him.*) Hey, cut that out!

Pops. Damned kids.

Neal. It was a cop.

Pops. Shut the door!

(B.J. *enters from alley wearing a raccoon coat.*)

B.J. What was that all about?

Neal. I was parking my cab and sprayed some cop with snow. Big deal.

B.J. (*To* Connie.) Hi sweetheart.

CONNIE. Hello, 'Mr. Gibson.'

B.J. Aw, don't start up with me again!

LOU. Ginger, get dressed. We gotta put some changes in your number in case Owen japs out on us tonight.

(*An enormous crash.* WALLY *has knocked something over out of our sight.*)

WALLY. No problem.

B.J. Owen's not coming tonight? (B.J. *goes Off to take off his coat.*)

GINGER. I made almost three dollars in tips tonight.

LOU. (*Impressed.*) Great. Sign in, B.J.

POPS. Don't track up my floor! That's it, I quit, Lou.

LOU. You can't quit, Pops, there's a war on.

(GINGER *crosses with a magazine.* NEAL *re-enters and checks his mail.*)

POPS. Hey, come back here with that magazine!

NEAL. (*Who has discovered a banana peel in his mailbox.*) Who put this in my box?

LOU. Where are you going?

GINGER. I gotta go potty.

LOU. Come on, Ginger. We gotta rehearse.

NEAL. (*Getting out his pipe.*) Hey, Pops, you mind if I smoke?

POPS. I don't care if you burn.

(NEAL *lights his pipe.*)

B.J. (*Re-entering. To* CONNIE.) Did you call your mom yet?

CONNIE. No.

B.J. Dog drat it, Connie. I thought I could at least count on you to call your own mother. Now I'm gonna get in a lot of trouble.

CONNIE. Good!

(CONNIE *exits Off Right.* B.J. *checks his mail, then goes into the anteroom and combs his hair.*)

POPS. Hey, you kids get out of here. This is my room.

NEAL. (*Pinching* WALLY'S *cheek.*) Wally Fergusson, who do you love, Wally?

WALLY. You, Mr. Tilden.

NEAL. What a guy, hey, Pops? Heh heh heh.

POPS. Get out of here.

NEAL. Hey, Wally, let's shake.

(*A routine. They stand apart and shiver exaggeratedly.*)

POPS. BEAT IT!

CLIFTON. (*Exploding out of his office.*) Goddammit!

LOU. B.J., Neal, give me a hand with these.

(*They help* LOU *set up chairs.* WALLY *wanders, getting in the way.* STANLEY *is on a ladder cabling a light.* ANN COLLIER *enters from the alley.*)

ANN. Hi, Pops.

POPS. (*Suddenly cheerful.*) Here she is.

ANN. Hi, everybody.

B.J. Hi, Ann.

POPS. I've got some fan mail for you here, I think. Let me help you with your coat.

ANN. (*Collapsing into* POPS' *chair, then puts her feet up on his desk and lights a cigarette.*) Thanks, Pops.

POPS. Want some coffee?

ANN. I'd kill for some coffee. I am beat to my socks. (*To* CLIFTON *who breezes by on the way back to his office.*) I'm sorry I'm late, Cliff. There aren't any cabs and I had to get home to find a sitter.

CLIFTON. Where's Cantone?

ANN. How should I know?

CONNIE. He was at the restaurant giving out autographs.

ANN. I bet.

POPS. (*To* CONNIE *who is drinking a Coke.*) You shouldn't drink that stuff. It eats through your stomach.

CLIFTON. Wait a minute, wait a minute. (*Silence.*) What is this? What is going on here? (*Looks around.*) Feet on desks? Standing on ladders? We go on the air in less than thirty minutes and everyone is fooling around? I mean the least you could do is rehearse. It's not like you don't need it. We are about to be broadcast into thousands of homes—doesn't that mean anything to any of you? I mean I'm sweating nickels up here. And is it too much to ask that you be here on time? Maybe it *is* too much to ask that you be here on time. Why should any of you be here on time? Why should any of you be here at all? You are fired, all of you! Will you get to work? This place isn't even set up yet. Cheese and crackers, will you look at those chairs? (*To* LOU.) Have you called Owen yet? No, I've got to do that. I've got to do everything. Leave it to Clifton. Nobody cares what happens tonight except me, I can see that. We go on the air in twenty-two minutes and we will never make it. You'd better call the transmitter and tell them we're going to be late. Or why don't we just cancel the whole show? Bring me a Bromo. Where's Wally with my coffee? And Goddammit, who put the gum in my typewriter? (*He exits Right in a huff. Pause.*)

WALLY. (*Quietly.*) Cheese and crackers?

ANN. It's an expression.

NEAL. Maybe he's hungry.

WALLY. Yeah.

LOU. Come on, you heard the man, let's get to work here. Move it move it move it move it!

POPS. Oh, shut up.

(ANN *gets the mail from* POPS *and starts looking at it.*)

LOU. (*Screaming down the Left hall.*) Ginger!
(GINGER *enters from the hall wearing a slip.*)
You gonna rehearse like that?

GINGER. Like what?

POPS. (*To* ANN.) You know I worked a lot of shows—I mean real shows, not this nickel and dime stuff. And nobody ever got this much mail.

ANN. Pops.

POPS. No, really.

CONNIE. Ginger, you gonna rehearse like that?

GINGER. Like what?
(CONNIE *begins to rehearse her tap.*)

POPS. (*To* ANN.) I even worked *Rainbow Rendezvous.*

ANN. You're kidding.

POPS. Well, it was out of Cleveland then, and I'd come out and do a sort of warm up number before the show . . .

LOU. Okay, good evening, ladies and gentlemen. Good evening, Ginger.

POPS. (*To* ANN.) 'Course, I was a lot younger then. .

LOU. We have to do a little shifting in Miss Brooks' number tonight.

GINGER. Yay!

LOU. Nothing to worry about, as Mr. Owen may not be with us this evening.

(Pops *is still entertaining* Ann, *who is laughing at his routines.*
    Connie *is Left, tapping her heart out.*)

Pops. (*Singing.*) "I guess I'll have to dream the rest . . ." (*He
continues singing under the scene.*)
    Wally. Owen's definitely not coming, Lou?
    Neal. Owen's not coming tonight?
    Lou. Nothing definite, we're waiting for a call.
    Wally. Lou.
    Neal. That lush.
    Lou. Wally, how about my hot chocolate? B.J., go get Zoot.
                    (B.J. *exits Left hall.*)
    Neal. Who's going to do his ballad? He's got a ballad.
    Wally. I can do those routines, Lou.
    Lou. Don't be ridiculous, Wally.
    Pops. (*To* Ann, *who is laughing.*) I even told jokes.
    Neal. Yeah, don't be a jerk.
    Pops. (*To* Ann.) No kidding.
    Neal. That ballad's in my key, Lou.
    Wally. I know all of his routines. I rehearsed all week when
no one was looking.
                (Ann *laughs at* Pops' *routine.*)
    Neal. E's my key, Lou.
    Wally. Please, Lou, please?
    Lou. It's not up to me.
    Wally. Watch this, Lou.
    Neal. Listen, Lou.

(Wally *dances around like Cagney, singing "I'M A YANKEE
    DOODLE DANDY" while* Neal *demonstrates his singing
    voice.* B.J. *enters from the Left hall in time for* Wally *to
    step on his foot.* B.J. *screams.*)

    Ginger. Come on, Lou, I'm getting cold.
    B.J. Wally, watch out.
    Neal. Let me do the ballad, Lou.
                    (*The pay phone rings.*)
    Pops. (*To* Ann, *on his way to answer the pay phone.*) *Thrifty
Drug Stores*, now there was a show . . .
    Wally. I can even do imitations.
    Neal. That ballad's got my name on it, Lou.
    Wally. "Wah, wah, wah, when you're old and grey dear . . ."
That's my Jimmy Stewart.

GINGER. Are we going to rehearse my number or not?

LOU. Ginger.

NEAL. Neal Tilden, Lou.

WALLY. (*Doing Bogart.*) "You know, Lou, there's other things in life besides dames."

LOU. Neal! Wally!

WALLY. (*Durante.*) "That's the name, I got a million of 'em."

LOU. Get off my back!

POPS. (*Stepping to the edge of the greenroom area.*) Wally, your uncle says that unless you make those deliveries within the next ten minutes, he's sending you back to Altoona.

WALLY. Yikes.

LOU. And don't forget the coffee and the hot chocolate.

WALLY. Right, Lou.

NEAL. Would you ask Clifton for me, Lou?

LOU. (*Emphatically.*) No. Now everyone, let's go to work.

(CLIFTON *enters from his office with the scripts.*)

CLIFTON. Okay, everybody, here are your scripts.

LOU. Take five, get your scripts.

(*All go to get their scripts which* CLIFTON *has dropped on a chair.*)

NEAL. Ask him, Lou! Ask him!

(ZOOT *enters from the Left hall with all of the music for the show.* B.J. *and* CONNIE *talk to* ZOOT *while he places the music on the music stands in the band stand.*)

ANN. Hey, Pops, can I use your phone?

POPS. Sure.

(*To* CLIFTON *as he passes through the greenroom and exits Off Right.*)

Hey, Cliff, I ever tell you about the time I did the warmup for *Rainbow Rendezvous*?

CLIFTON. No.

POPS. (*Following* CLIFTON *Off.*) Well, we were coming out of Cleveland, you see, and I'd come out and do this number . . .

(LOU *plays the piano and* GINGER *rehearses her dance.*)

B.J. (*Looking at a sheet of music. To* ZOOT *who is still busy at work.*) Really? A-Flat?

ANN. (*Into phone.*) Don Sterling, please. Ann Collier calling.

STANLEY. (*About to put a gel into a lighting instrument.*) Hey, Mr. Cohn, you want amber in this?

LOU. (*Preoccupied with* GINGER'S *rehearsal.*) Amber's swell.

STANLEY. I don't have any amber.

CONNIE. (*To* ZOOT.) I sound better in A-Flat.

B.J. Who says?

ZOOT. Her mom.

(ZOOT *goes to the piano.*)

LOU. Ginger, wait a minute.

GINGER. Can't we quit till the fellas come? I'm getting all sweaty.

LOU. No. Zoot, help me out will you?

(ZOOT *begins playing an undistinguishable melody—a dance break to* "BLUES IN THE NIGHT"—*to which* LOU *demonstrates a very complicated and gymnastic and very feminine bit of choreography. Silly because he's doing it. Other* MUSICIANS *join in. All are watching and laughing. When it's over, All applaud.* LOU *is embarrassed but takes the applause with smiles.*)

CLIFTON. Okay, everybody, starting next week the call is one hour before air time. Anyone not inside that door by eight o'clock will be locked out.

(*As he starts to cross back to his office,* NEAL *stops him.* ZOOT *works with* CONNIE *and* B.J. *at the piano on* "HOW ABOUT YOU".)

NEAL. Cliff, Cliff, don't get all testy. I got it all worked out. If Owen doesn't show up, I'll do the ballad and Wally can do the little junk.

CLIFTON. Owen will show up, Neal.

NEAL. What if he doesn't? Clifton, please?

(CLIFTON *exits into his office,* NEAL *follows.* GENEVA *enters from the alley with two or three of her musicians who also play in* ZOOT'S *band.*)

GENEVA. Okay, ya'll, we can start, I am here.

LOU. Geneva, the call was 8:30.

GENEVA. Child, we play other gigs.

LOU. You're still late.

GENEVA. You're still fat.

(CLIFTON *re-enters.* NEAL *still tagging along.* NEAL *is brushing off his knees.*)

CLIFTON. Neal, get up. I can't make promises like that. Lou, did you get Owen? Geneva, you're late.

LOU. (*Writing something on his clipboard.*) He was taking a bath.

CLIFTON. (*Going back into his office.*) Judas Priest. (*Slams door.*)

GENEVA. (*Playing the piano while she speaks.*) Last night, Curtis and Izzy and I went down and tried to get into the club. They had this big, ugly sucker at the door, and he came up to me and said, "Who do you think you are, Lena Horne?" and I said no, but that I knew Miss Horne like a sister and she told me the next time I was in town to come on down and look her up. And he said why didn't I say so in the first place, 'cause, wouldn't you know, she was there? Now, honey, I ain't never laid eyes on Lena Horne, but when that guy came back, he said come on in! Honey not only was I pretending that *I* knew *her* . . . she was pretending that *she* knew *me!*

(GENEVA *plays and some of the* MUSICIANS *join in.*)

Well, the next thing you know, it was Lena this and Harold that, and have you met the Duke, he's right over there, and the place was jumpin' and jivin'. Wooo, this sounds good!

(They play loud. "Bop." CLIFTON *enters from his office.*)

CLIFTON. (*Yelling over the music.*) Hey, Lou, any word from Owen?

LOU. Not yet.

CLIFTON. How about Cantone? And Biff?

LOU. What?

CLIFTON. Cantone!

LOU. Geneva, knock it off. I can't hear myself think.

CONNIE. Everyone, please! I am on the phone!

(*Screams from outside. Flashbulbs flash.* CANTONE *enters from the alley.*)

JOHNNY. Another dull night on the street.

(*They all react.* ANN *gets up and exits to the Left hall.* JOHNNY *grabs* NEAL'S *cheek in a big pinch.*)

Neal Tilden. Who do you love, Neal?

NEAL. You, Johnny.

(JOHNNY *slaps* NEAL'S *cheek.* NEAL *rubs it.*)

JOHNNY. What a guy. What a guy. (*He gives* CONNIE *his coat.*) Hey, sweetie, when are we going out for that drink?

B.J. Hey, Johnny.

JOHNNY. B.J. Gibson, what a guy. Hey, Ginger, you left your watch on my dressing table.

GINGER. (*As she breezes by into the greenroom.*) Dry up.

JOHNNY. Mind if I undress?

LOU. Johnny, we have dressing rooms.

JOHNNY. (*With a big smile.*) Really? Thanks, Lou.

GENEVA. Hey, you get lost last night? I thought you were gonna meet me down at the club?

JOHNNY. Yeah, well, I was detained. Oh, Lou, take care of our friends out there, would you?

(JOHNNY *gives* LOU *the last of the bills in his money clip.* LOU *takes them reluctantly.*)

LOU. I'm not your messenger boy. (LOU *exits to the alley.*)

JOHNNY. Thanks, Lou. (*To* WALLY.) He's a real guy, isn't he, Wally?

(WALLY *smiles.*)

POPS. (*At his desk. As* LOU *passes by,* POPS *looks to* GINGER *who is reading a magazine in the greenroom opposite him.*) Hey, keep those in order. How're we gonna know who's winning the war?

GINGER. (*Putting the magazine down. To* CONNIE *who is standing there with* JOHNNY'S *coat.*) I wish they had more articles on dating and shyness; this war stuff is really boring.

(POPS *is tuning the radio on his desk to find another station.*)

CONNIE. (*Still holding* CANTONE'S *coat.*) I think he's gorgeous.

GINGER. I think he's grody.

WALLY. Mr. Cantone?

JOHNNY. Not now, Wally.

(ANN *comes into the studio from the Left hall.* JOHNNY *sees her.*) Hey, Collier.

ANN. I told you. I don't want to talk about it.

JOHNNY. Come on.

(JOHNNY *goes over to her and they begin a private conversation.*)

POPS. (*About a radio show he's listening to.*) Hey, listen to this.

(WALLY *wanders over.*)

GINGER. What's all the screaming about, that's what I'd like to know.

NEAL. (*Confidentially.*) He pays 'em.

GINGER. (*Still talking to* CONNIE *who is not listening.*) I wouldn't even scream for Sinatra, and *he* sends me right to the cinema.

NEAL. (*To* GINGER *who isn't listening.*) He pays 'em to scream, I bet.

POPS. (*Laughs at something on the radio.*) Did you hear that? (*Laughs again.* WALLY *laughs half-heartedly.*)

GINGER. (*Going through her purse.*) I mean why would a girl want to open her mouth real big and scream at a fella she'd like to go out with.

(POPS *laughs at the radio.* WALLY *wanders.* CONNIE *is still holding* JOHNNY'S *coat.* NEAL *is looking out the window.* B.J. *is practicing a dance step for "HOW ABOUT YOU."* GENEVA *is playing the piano softly—something bluesy, some other instruments join in.* ZOOT *is leaning on the piano listening.* JOHNNY *and* ANN *are now arguing.*)

Suppose she had something on her teeth?

NEAL. (*Turning around.*) Ginger, he *does* pay 'em.

GINGER. (*To* NEAL.) Teeth are very important.

NEAL. What?

GINGER. (*Cheerfully.*) And so is your makeup. (*She begins to put on lipstick.*)

NEAL. No, no. Cantone pays 'em. He pays 'em to scream. (A beat.) I wonder how much?

(*The desk phone rings.* POPS *puts his cigar in his mouth— something he always does to answer the phones.* NEAL *sinks down on* POPS' *desk to think.*)

POPS. (*To* NEAL.) Get off my desk. (*Into phone.*) WOV, New York City, may I help you?

(NEAL *gets up and goes to get some coffee. Someone has put a Baby Ruth wrapper in his mug.*)

LOU. (*Entering from the outside, shaking off the cold.*) Brrr!

NEAL. Who put this in my mug?

POPS. I got a tip on Blonde Boy in the second.

LOU. I thought you only took those on the pay phone.

POPS. I needed two lines.

GINGER. (*About her lipstick.*) Thick and perfect.

Lou. Okay, everybody, let's get to work on Ginger's number.

Pops. (*Writing down the bet on the wall next to the pay phone. To* Neal.) Go easy on that coffee, Pal.

Johnny. Oh, come on, we worked all afternoon on Ginger's number.

Lou. Well, we're going to work a little more.

Ginger. (*Going Off down the Left hall.*) I gotta go potty, Lou.

Lou. (*Exasperated.*) Take Five. (Lou *goes Off after* Ginger.)

Neal. (*Into the pay phone.*) Hi. Could I speak to Ray Owen, please? No no no, don't get him! Just tell him that Clifton called and not to bother coming down to the station tonight 'cause there's been a fire. (*He hangs up.*)

Wally. Mr. Cantone?

Johnny. Not now, Wally.

Wally. Mr. Tilden?

Neal. (*Having just committed a mortal sin.*) Not now, Wally.

Wally. (*To himself.*) I might get to go on tonight.

Johnny. Hey, Pops, who's running?

Pops. (*Coming back to his desk with a cup of coffee.*) No.

Johnny. Come on. Who do you love, Pops?

Pops. Cut that out! That stuff doesn't work with me.

Johnny. Two bucks, Pops. I'm good for it.

Pops. Not till you've paid up.

Johnny. Geneva, can you loan me two bucks?

Geneva. No.

Johnny. Hey, Collier.

Ann. No.

Zoot. No.

(Pops' *radio still plays.*)

Johnny. (*Sees* Neal *standing by the coffee machine.*) Neal Tilden, what a guy, what a guy. (*Pinches* Neal's *cheek like always.*)

Neal. (*Smiling through the pain.*) Hey, Johnny.

Johnny. You got a couple of bucks I can borrow?

Neal. Two *dollars*?

Johnny. Well, I just—oh, never mind.

Neal. (*Curious.*) What?

Johnny. No, I shouldn't be talking about it. Nobody knows yet.

Neal. (*The magic words.*) What?

JOHNNY. Well, I'm going away tomorrow and I'm gonna need all the cash I can lay my hands on.

NEAL. Where are you going?

JOHNNY. (*Looks around before speaking.*) Movies.

NEAL. (*Doesn't understand.*) You're going to the movies?

JOHNNY. No, no. *Mo*vies.

NEAL. (*Understands.*) Oh, you're going to the *mo*vies.

JOHNNY. (*Shaking his head.*) Uh uh. (*A beat.*) Hollywood.

NEAL. You're going to Hollywood?

JOHNNY. Shhh.

NEAL. (*Quietly.*) You're going to Hollywood?

(JOHNNY *nods.*)

But how can you go to Hollywood and do this show too?

(JOHNNY *shakes his head.*)

You're *not* going to Hollywood.

(JOHNNY *shakes his head again.*)

You're not going to do this sh—you're not going to do this show?

JOHNNY. Shhh.

NEAL. (*Almost inaudible.*) Wow.

JOHNNY. Anyway, Clifton's gonna need a new featured vocalist. And I don't have to tell you what a word from me would do. You've got seniority and everything.

NEAL. (*Going to heaven.*) Featured vocalist?

JOHNNY. Now I can't promise anyth—

NEAL. (*In heaven.*) Featured vocalist.

JOHNNY. Two bucks.

NEAL. (*In a trance.*) Two bucks.

JOHNNY. So I can get to Hollywood.

NEAL. Right. Two bucks so you can get to Hollywood. (NEAL *gets the money from his clip purse. Starts to give it to* JOHNNY *but withholds it and suddenly gets serious. The condition.*) You'll talk to Clifton.

JOHNNY. (*Taking the money.*) Would I let you down? You just make this the best show you've ever done.

NEAL. (*Grimly. Plotting.*) Right. (*Starts to make a phone call on the pay phone.*)

ANN. (*Who has been listening. To* JOHNNY.) You creep.

JOHNNY. You love it. Okay, Pops, who's running? (JOHNNY *starts to place the bet with* POPS. *The desk phone rings. It is* NEAL *calling from the pay phone.*)

POPS. WOV, New York City. Can I help you?

NEAL. (*Into phone, concealing his voice with a handkerchief.*)
Ray Owen.

POPS. What?

NEAL. Ray Owen.

POPS. Who *is* this?

NEAL. (*Loud and clear.*) Ray Owen!

POPS. Don't move from that phone, Buster. Clifton's gonna
want to speak to you. Hey, Wally, go tell Clifton Ray Owen's on
the phone. Hurry up!

(WALLY *runs into* CLIFTON'S *office.* LOU *re-enters from Left.*
NEAL *speaks to* CLIFTON *on the phone as* RAY OWEN. *We
don't hear the conversation.*)

LOU. Okay, could I work with the gentlemen first please?
Johnny, B.J., Neal? All right, if Ray Owen is absent we'll need
to condense the four-man routine into a three-man routine.

JOHNNY. Oh, come on!

WALLY. I know that routine, Lou.

LOU. Wally!

JOHNNY. Right, Lou. Let Wally fill in. He's a trouper, aren't
you Wally? Come on, be a guy.

B.J. You just don't want to rehearse.

JOHNNY. B.J. Gibson, what a guy.

(NEAL *hangs up. Wipes fingerprints off the receiver.*)

CLIFTON. (*Coming out of his office.*) Wait a minute, Lou. It
looks like Owen's not coming. Something about a fire. Neal?

NEAL. (*Innocent.*) Yes?

CLIFTON. Owen's not coming. So I guess you'll have to sing the
ballad.

LOU. What? Clifton?

WALLY. (*Following* CLIFTON *and* LOU *into the office.*) Mr. Feddington? What about Wally Fergusson? Let me do something
too. Come on, nobody'll know . . .

NEAL. Well, everyone, it looks like Clifton recognized my
talent, which is sizeable, and I finally got that ballad I deserve.

(ZOOT *hands* NEAL *the arrangement.*)

ZOOT. Here, Neal.

NEAL. (*Full of himself.*) Oh. Thank you Zoot. (*Looks at it.*)
Ahhh. I'll just look over the arrangement briefly. Maybe I can
make a few suggestions later.

(WALLY *rushes On from* CLIFTON'S *office.*)

WALLY. I'm going on! I'm going on! Isn't that great? Wait'll I tell my Aunt. I can't believe it, I'm going on! Wooo! I'm going on.

(*He dashes out the alley door, almost mowing* BIFF *down, who enters immediately in uniform.*)

BIFF. I hear he's going on.
POPS. (*Standing.*) Biff!
BIFF. You like my new suit?
                (*A mad dash to the greenroom.*)
LOU. Sign in, Biff. I'll get your coat. (LOU *takes his coat—Off Right.*)
JOHNNY. Hey, Biff, you look like you could use a drink. Let's you and me and Collier here go down to my dressing room.
BIFF. Don't we have a radio show or something?
JOHNNY. To hell with the show. It'll be like old times.
ANN. Biff, you look great.
BIFF. I told you I would.
LOU. Johnny, get dressed.
BIFF. Atta boy, Lou.
NEAL. (*Full of himself.*) Biff!
CONNIE. Hi, Biff.
BIFF. (*Swinging her around.*) Hi, Sweetie.
CONNIE. You look swell.
BIFF. Thanks.
NEAL. (*Arm out-stretched.*) Biff!
BIFF. Hi, B.J.
GENEVA. Hey, soldier boy. (WALLY *re-enters from alley with a few more deliveries.*)
BIFF. Hi, Geneva. Hi, Mr. Doubleman.
WALLY. Hey, Biff, I'm going on.
BIFF. (*To* ANN.) He is?
CLIFTON. (*Over the loudspeaker, from booth.*) Alright, could I have everybody's attention?
LOU. Listen up, everybody. (*Everyone faces Upstage to* CLIFTON, *above, in the booth.* STANLEY *is in the booth with* CLIFTON, *and is eating a sandwich.*)
CLIFTON. (*Seriously.*) Tonight is a special night. As every night's a special night. We have a show to do, and we're gonna do it well. We have to come in on time and we have to be sharp. Now this week's rehearsal will pay off if everyone thinks and keeps awake.

Lou. You gotta be good tonight.

Clifton. Thank you, Lou. Our studio audience is outside. We have less than ten minutes. Let 'em in, Lou.

(Lou *becomes Mr. Officious. He addresses the house manager as well as those Onstage, and bustles around constantly. The orchestra tunes up for the first time, then* Zoot *rehearses the Quintet for "I'LL NEVER SMILE AGAIN," the Cast also bustle around, ad libbing to each other, and notice the audience as if for the first time.*)

Lou. (*Screaming into the house.*) Okay, Freddy, let 'em in. Oh, Christ! (*To the Cast.*) Places please, Studio B, places everyone places, please. Get 'em in here quick, Freddy. We're about to go on the air, everyone (*Screaming down the Left hall.*) Johnny, get dressed. (*Tapping at* Clifton's *door.*) We're assembling Mr. Feddington. (*Blows a whistle he has around his neck.*) Places, everybody. Zoot, knock it off. Neal, B.J., help me with these chairs.

(Neal *and* B.J. *help move the chairs into position.* Stanley *is flashing different lights on and off from his Onstage dimmer controls.*)

Wally, where are you going?

Wally. I want to get my good pants.

Lou. This is radio, Wally.

(*Hollering suddenly.* Pops *is on the phone, placing the bets.*) Let's go, let's go, let's go, let's go. There are still some empty seats down here, Freddy. Pops, get off the phone. (*To the audience.*) Hi, folks, thanks for braving the storm. (*Angry suddenly.*) Musicians, if you haven't tuned up now, it is too late. (*About* Geneva's *coat.*) Geneva, is this yours?

Geneva. Of course it's mine, chrome dome.

Lou. Geneva—

Stanley. (*Over loud speaker.*) Only about a minute, Mr. Cohn.

Wally. Lou, do I have time to call my aunt?

Lou. No, you do not have time to call your aunt, this is show business. (*To an audience member down front.*) Hey, Buster, no orange peels on the floor.

(B.J. *and* Connie *are down front and are pointing to supposed audience members they recognize and call them by name.* Lou *reads from a scrap of paper.*)

Ladies and gentlemen, there will be no regular bus service back to Jersey tonight because of the storm, however, there will be one bus which will leave twenty minutes after the show tonight

which can drop you in any of the cities on the list at the back of
the house. Thank you. (*Suddenly screaming.*) Let's go. Move it
move it move it move it. (*All is still chaos.*) Whose script is this?
Whose script is this? Let's go. (*Shouting down the hall.*) Cantone, we are waiting for you!

(JOHNNY *enters and tosses his hat on the piano. There is a drum
roll. Suddenly, on the cymbal crash, everyone is in place:
the Performers are seated in their chairs in the studio,
GENEVA is on a stool in front of the Band, CANTONE standing
mid-Stage, LOU is alert to cue STANLEY, ZOOT and CLIFTON
and is watching the clock and his stopwatch. JOHNNY is in a
tux, smoking a cigarette and drinking from a Manhattan
glass. Follow spot hits CLIFTON. He smiles at the audience.
A chat before the show.*)

CLIFTON. (*Addressing the audience as the 'studio' audience.*)
Good evening to you, ladies and gentlemen of our studio au-
dience.
(*It's a miracle that all has come together this quickly. The clock
now says about two minutes to nine.*)
Just a few more moments now until air time. I'd like to take this
opportunity to introduce a few of the familiar faces here in the
WOV radio family. First of all, our special Christmas show this
year marks the last show for the youngest member of our band.
Welcome will you, fourth trumpet and Second Lieutenant, Biff
Baker. Biff, take a bow.

(BIFF *approaches the microphone.*)

BIFF. Hi, folks. Thanks.

(CANTONE *tries to kid with* BIFF *about something as he makes his
way back to the Band.*)

CLIFTON. Biff is a member of the most versatile band in the
land, the Zoot Doubleman Orchestra. Zoot, take a bow.
(ZOOT *stands. The Drummer starts a drum roll, and the follows
hit* ZOOT *who milks the applause, gestures to the Band, cues
the cymbal crash and the follows return to* CLIFTON. *LOU
gives last minute instructions to* ZOOT *who makes some notes
on his music.* LOU *is clocking all of this and watching the
second hands of the studio clocks. The Performers are adjusting scripts, listening to* CLIFTON, *applauding when they
think of it, and are otherwise nervous about the broadcast.*

WALLY FERGUSSON *is standing behind* CLIFTON, *inching up closer to the mic and, at* NEAL'S *prompting, is shining his shoes on the backs of his trouser legs, making sure his fly is zipped up and smoothing down his hair.*)

Well, folks, as you know, Ray Owen hasn't been with us for several weeks now, and, as of tonight, probably won't be with us much longer. Our replacement for Ray tonight will be Neal Tilden in the solo spot,

(NEAL *stands and waves.*)

and with the Boutineers, our delivery boy from Piccadilly Drug Store, Mr. Wally Fergusson.

(*The audience applauds. The Cast too.* NEAL *is standing.* WALLY *approaches the microphone. Humble.*)

WALLY. Hello. How are you?

(WALLY *gets pulled away from the microphone by* LOU. NEAL *is laughing at him.* NEAL *pulls* WALLY *down into his seat and tells him he made a fool of himself.* LOU *tells him to shut-tup.* CLIFTON *continues.*)

CLIFTON. (*Laughing a little.*) Thank you, Wally. Keep those deliveries coming.

LOU. (*Getting a cue on headset. Watching the clock.*) Thirty-five seconds.

CLIFTON. Now folks, when you see the "On The Air" signs flash . . .

(*They do.*)

LOU. Thirty seconds. Stand by.

(*The "Stand By" signs light up and stay lit.*)

ZOOT. (*To the Band.*) Stand by.

CLIFTON. . . . Thank you, Lou; we will be broadcasting live tonight. December 21, 1942 courtesy of the Atlantic Coast Network here in New York City. Now folks, you in our studio audience will be privileged to see things tonight that our audiences at home do not see. For them, and for the boys overseas who will hear this program on shortwave tonight, boys who would like to know that all is well in America, please respond accordingly when you see these signs illuminate.

(*The "Applause" sign flashes three times.* CLIFTON *watches* LOU *with his hand cupped over his hear.* LOU *is taking visual and verbal cues from* STANLEY *in the booth who is scurrying around taking cues from someone at the transmitter on a phone. He signals numbers to* LOU *who quietly counts off to* CLIFTON.)

LOU. Five, four, three, two. [MUSIC NO. 1 "KALAMA ZOO"] (*Lou points to* ZOOT. *The Band starts a fanfare.* LOU *points to* CLIFTON *at the first break.*)

CLIFTON. (*Excitedly.*) Live from the Algonquin Room of the Beautiful Hotel Astor on the lovely Times Square in New York. (*The Band begins to play "KALAMAZOO." Under the instrumental:*)
It's nine o'clock in New York and time for the Atlantic Coast Network to present WOV's Mutual Manhattan Variety Cavalcade! (*The "Applause" signs flash twice.* LOU *cues the audience to applaud by waving his arm around his head, then fades the applause.*)
Thank you, thank you, you're very kind. That's right, another sparkling hour of music and song, comedy and drama with the Feddington Players, featuring Zoot Doublemand and his orchestra, and Johnny Cantone and his family of All Stars! (*The "Applause" signs flash twice.*)
Thank you. Featuring Ann Collier, (*They each wave to the audience at the mention of their names.*) Geneva Lee Browne, Neal Tilden, B.J. Gibson and Connie Miller, Ginger Brooks, introducing Wally Fergusson. (WALLY *pokes someone in case they hadn't heard.* CLIFTON *adds, humbly:*) Clifton Feddington, speaking.

(*The Company sings "I GOT A GAL FROM KALAMAZOO."* CLIFTON *sings lead, the Whole Group backs him up. Just before the playoff, the phone rings.* POPS *gets it, coming out of an argument we don't hear with* LOU. *It's for* WALLY. WALLY *knows it's for* WALLY. *He goes to answer it. And keeps singing as he goes. In the greenroom, he puts on his flatcap with "Piccadilly Drug Store" embroidered on the side and takes down some info on his checkbook. Now he crosses back to sing the last snatches of the song in the center mic.* POPS *badgers to get going.*)

CHORUS.
HI, THERE, CLIFF, HOW'S YOUR NEW ROMANCE?
THE ONE YOU MET AT THE CAMPUS DANCE.
CLIFTON.
WAIT UNTIL YOU SEE HER, YOU'LL AGREE.

MY HOMETOWN GAL'S THE ONLY GAL FOR ME.
A-B-C-D-E-F-G-H-I GOT A GAL
   CHORUS.
IN KALAMAZOO.
   CLIFTON.
DON'T WANNA BOAST, BUT I KNOW SHE'S THE TOAST
   CHORUS.
OF KALAMAZOO, ZOO, ZOO, ZOO, ZOO, ZOO.
   CLIFTON.
YEARS HAVE GONE BY
   CHORUS.
MY, MY HOW SHE GREW.
   CLIFTON.
I LIKED HER LOOKS, WHEN I CARRIED HER BOOKS
   CHORUS.
IN KALAMAZOO, ZOO, ZOO, ZOO, ZOO.
   CLIFTON.
I'M GONNA SEND A WIRE,
HOPPIN' ON A FLYER,
   CHORUS.
LEAVIN' TODAY.
   CLIFTON.
AM I DREAMIN',
I CAN HEAR HER SCREAMIN',
   CHORUS.
"HIYA, MISTER JACKSON"
EVERYTHING'S O.K-A-L-A-M-A-Z-O-O
   MEN.
OH, WHAT A GAL,
   CHORUS.
A REAL PIPPEROO.
   CLIFTON.
I'LL MAKE MY BID FOR THAT FRECKLED FACE KID
I'M HURRYIN' TO
   MEN.
I'M GOIN' TO MICHIGAN
TO SEE THE SWEETEST GAL
   CHORUS.
IN KALAMAZOO.
   CLIFTON.
K.
   CHORUS.
K.

CLIFTON.

A.

CHORUS.

A. L-A-M-A-Z-O-O OH, OH, OH WHAT A GAL
A REAL PIPPEROO!

CLIFTON.

I'LL MAKE MY BID FOR THAT FRECKLED FACE KID
I'M HURRYIN' TO.

CHORUS.

WE'RE GOIN' TO MICHIGAN
TO SEE THE SWEETEST GAL IN KALAMAZOO.
ZOO-ZOO-ZOO-ZOO-ZOO!
KALAMAZOO!

(*Instrumental playoff. The "Applause" signs flash. The Company breaks away, ad lib dancing, from the microphones to their next places.* WALLY *starts out. Says a hundred goodbyes to* CANTONE *who could care less.* POPS *gives* ANN *a Christmas present. A corsage which she eventually puts on. Lots of scurrying around.* LOU *gets the next people on the deck and ready to go. The lighting onstage is now deeply colored and saturated.* CLIFTON *tries to get an order into* WALLY *before he leaves. Music ends, "Applause" signs flash.*)

CLIFTON. (*Truly excited.*) Thank you, thank you and good evening, everyone, and thanks for tuning in. Of course that was Warren and Gordon's brand new hit kicking off our potpourri of music and song.

[MUSIC NO. 3 "PEPSI COLA"]

(*The Band begins "PEPSI COLA."* NEAL, B.J., CONNIE *and* GINGER *assemble at the center mic,* CLIFTON *at side,* LOU *at the sound effects table.*)

CONNIE.

NICKEL

B.J.

NICKEL

BOTH.

TOO DOO DEE AH DAH

WOMEN.

NICKEL

MEN.
NICKEL
ALL.
TOO DOO DEE AHT 'N' DAH BAH
PEPSI COLA HITS THE SPOT
TWELVE FULL OUNCES, THAT'S A LOT
TWICE 'Z MUCH FOR A NICKEL TOO
PEPSI COLA IS THE DRINK FOR YOU.
DOOT DOOT DOOT, etc.

(NEAL *grabs* CONNIE'S *Coke bottle away from her.* CLIFTON *speaks and* LOU *performs the sound effects: the "qwish" and ice cubes.*)

CLIFTON. (*Speaking over.*) Ummm, Mmmm. Listen to that. The sound of Pepsi Cola on ice. Do what thousands of soldiers do every day. Pop a top on a Pepsi and you'll agree with the Boutineers.
CONNIE & GINGER.
NICKEL, NICKEL, NICKEL, NICKEL
B.J. & NEAL.
TRICKLE, TRICKLE, TRICKLE, TRICKLE
ALL.
NICKEL, NICKEL, NICKEL, NICKEL
YAH DAHH DAH DAH

ALL.	CLIFTON.
PAH!	PAH!

[MUSIC NO. 4 "DADDY"]
(*The Band starts the intro to "DADDY".*)
BAND. (*Singing.*)
LA DA DA, LA DA DA, DA DA DA
LA DA DA, LA DA DA, DA DA DA
LA DA DA, LA DA DA, DA DA DA
DA DA DA DA DA DA DA DA, DA DA DA

HEY LISTEN
TO MY STORY 'BOUT
A GAL NAMED DAISY MAE
LAZY DAISY MAE

HER DISPOSITION
IS RATHER SWEET AND CHARMING
AT TIMES ALARMING
SO THEY SAY

DA DA DA DA DA, DA DA DA
DA DA DA DA DA, DA DA DA

SHE HAD A MAN, RICH,
TALL, DARK, HANDSOME,
LARGE AND STRONG

TO WHOM SHE USED TO SING THIS SONG

CLIFTON. (*Speaking over.*) Here's a newcomer to WOV's Cavalcade—fresh off the bus from Ogden, Utah—came to New York—met B.J. and, well, the rest is history. Cute litte Connie Miller.

(JOHNNY *watches* CONNIE *lasciviously. Gives her a wink.*)

CONNIE. (*Sings.*)
HEY, DADDY
I WANT A DIAMOND RING, BRACELETS, EVERYTHING,
DADDY
YOU OUGHTA GET THE BEST FOR ME, YA, YA, YA,
HEY DADDY, GEE
WON'T I LOOK SWELL IN SABLES
CLOTHES WITH PARIS LABELS
DADDY, YOU OUGHTA GET THE BEST FOR ME
HERE'S 'N AMAZING REVELATION
WITH A BIT OF STIMULATION
I'D BE A GREAT SENSATION
I'D BE YOUR INSPIRATION
DADDY
I WANT A BRAND NEW CAR, CHAMPAGNE, CAVIAR
DADDY
YOU OUGHTA GET THE BEST FOR ME.

(*Band break.* WALLY *comes in from outside with more deliveries. Brings* CLIFTON *his coffee.* CLIFTON *tries to pay.* WALLY *refuses.* WALLY *is standing there pulling up his socks, holding a bag of deliveries which he sets in the greenroom, and which pile up during the broadcast. He decides to present* CONNIE *with a hot dog, partially unwrapped. She looks at it, holds it, smiles and gives it back to him. He shrugs his*

shoulders and takes it back and takes a big bite out of it.
Connie *continues the song in Pig Latin.* Neal *is lost.*)

Connie.
AH HEY, ADDY DAY
Band.
DADDY
Connie.
I WANNA IAMOND DAY ING RAY, ACELETS BRAY
EVERY A ING THAY
ADDY DAY
Band.
DADDY
Connie.
OO YAY OUGHTAY ET GAY EST BAY OR FAY ME
AH HEY, ADDY DAY
Band.
DADDY
Connie.
WON'T I LOOK ELL SWAY IN ABLE SAY OTHES CLAY
WITH ARIS PAY ABELS LAY
ADDY DAY
Band.
DADDY
Connie.
ADDY DAY
Band.
DADDY
Connie.
YOU OUGHTTA GET THE BEST FOR ME. DOO WAH!

(*"Applause" signs flash at the end of the number,* Ann, Connie *and* Neal *have assembled at the left mic to sing the call letters. The Drummer strikes the chimes.* Ann *is trying to get* Wally *to come over—he's supposed to be in this.* Lou *grabs him after having cued* Ginger *for her ad and pushes him up to the mic where he sings the signature with a mouthful of hot dog.*)

[MUSIC NO. 4A "W.O.U. STATION I"]

Group. (*Singing.*) W—O—V—

CLIFTON. WOV-for-Victory time is nine (*Chime.*) Ten.

(WALLY *hides the hot dog behind his back. Then walks away eating it. Offers it so somebody in the Band.*)

GINGER. (*Stepping up to the mic after straightening her stockings.*) Say, Clifton?
CLIFTON. Ginger Brooks, ladies and gentlemen.

(*The "Applause" signs flash.* LOU *has told* WALLY *to put away the hot dog.* WALLY *nods and sticks it in his jacket pocket.* LOU *rushes up to encourage the audience's applause.*)

GINGER. Hi folks. (*Confidentially and with a pout.*) Say, Cliff? Have you noticed how popular Ann is over there?
                    (ANN *is standing alone.*)
CLIFTON. I'll say.
GINGER. Well, what's she got that I haven't got, Clifton?
CLIFTON. Well, that's easy, Ginger. She's discovered how to adorn her skin with a fragrance men love and combat body odor at the same time.
GINGER. You mean there's a nice-smelling soap a girl can depend on to protect her against offending?
CLIFTON. I'll say, Ginger. Cashmere Bouquet. You'll revel in its rich, cleansing suds that banish body odor forever by actual test.
GINGER. Thanks for the tip, Clifton. I'm going to go pick up a half dozen cakes right now.

(*She backs away from the mic, puts the gum back in her mouth, and smiles. She gets her purse from One of the Girls and heads Off towards the bathroom, waving as she goes. She says something to* LOU *as she goes and he just nods as he checks his stopwatch and then writes something down on his clipboard. They continue through the double doors together,* LOU *talking to her.* CLIFTON *continues.* ZOOT *is talking to One of the Musicians as* LOU *re-enters and rushes over to tell* ZOOT *of the time crunch.*)

CLIFTON. You just go do that, Ginger. Folks, smell that soap before you buy it and you'll instinctively prefer Cashmere Bouquet toilet soap. In green, pink or handsome white.
(*The Band starts playing* JOHNNY'S *Theme: a smoky cocktail piano chord progression that rambles around the hint of a melody.* JOHNNY *swaggers up to the mic, waving to the audience.* CLIFTON *speaks with reverence.*)

Ladies and gentlemen, the moment you've all been waiting for. Our featured vocalist tonight. Johnny Cantone. Johnny?

(*The "Applause" signs flash.* JOHNNY *is smoking a cigarette.*)

JOHNNY. I'd like to dedicate this number to my wife. (*Smirk.*) Wherever she is.

[MUSIC NO. 5 "LOVE IS HERE TO STAY"]

(*The Band vamps his song. He steps back from the mic to take a drag on his cigarette.*

The Band plays "LOVE IS HERE TO STAY." JOHNNY *sings with a voice like velvet. After the first phrase, the "Applause" signs flash and* JOHNNY *nods to their acknowledgement. He dips the mic to the sides during the number gracefully, playing to the Girls in the audience. As he does,* B.J. *practices the same moves, almost subconsciously.* WALLY *is watching entranced.* NEAL *is pure jealousy and irritated that* WALLY *is so intrigued.* CONNIE *is in love. So is* ANN.)

JOHNNY. (*Sings.*)
IT'S VERY CLEAR
OUR LOVE IS HERE TO STAY

(*"Applause" signs flash.*)

NOT FOR A YEAR
BUT EVER AND A DAY
THE RADIO AND THE TELEPHONE
AND THE MOVIES THAT WE KNOW
MAY BE PASSING FANCIES
AND IN TIME MAY GO
BUT OH, MY DEAR
OUR LOVE IS HERE TO STAY
TOGETHER WE'RE
GOING A LONG, LONG WAY
IN TIME THE ROCKIES MAY CRUMBLE
GIBRALTAR MAY TUMBLE
THEY'RE ONLY MADE OF CLAY
BUT OUR LOVE IS HERE TO STAY

(*Band break.* JOHNNY *steps away from mic, smokes and winks at the audience. Picks a bit of tobacco off his tongue.*)

IN TIME THE ROCKIES MAY CRUMBLE
GIBRALTAR MAY TUMBLE
THEY'RE ONLY MADE OF CLAY
BUT OUR LOVE IS HERE TO STAY

(*"Applause" signs flash. At the end of the number, WALLY applauds wildly, whistling, rushing up to JOHNNY to shake his hand. Follows him around. JOHNNY barely gets away from him, but WALLY is so wound up about how good he was, he continues talking about his performance even after CANTONE has left the stage—to whomever is standing there. NEAL is on his way to the center mic for the next ad. LOU rushes over to get B.J. NEAL waves WALLY away like whatever he is talking about isn't a big deal. B.J. and CLIFTON join NEAL at the center mic.*)

NEAL. (*Groaning.*) Ohhhh. Ohhhhh.
          (*All Three turn a page.*)
Ohhhhhh.

CLIFTON. Wake up needing a laxative? Let's look in on Frank one morning.

NEAL. (*Miserable, low voice.*) Boy do I need a laxative. Oh gosh, I'm trying a court case this morning, I'll have to postpone it, I can't go running out during the trial.

CLIFTON. Well, Frank put off needed relief.

NEAL. Ohh.

CLIFTON. So, troubled by constipation symptoms, he loses his temper, and the case.

B.J. Guilty.

NEAL. Oh, no.

CLIFTON. (*Cheerily.*) Bert, on the other hand, was just as smart as he could be. He took speedy Sal Hepatica. He had to go to court too, this morning, but he knew he had to go *before* he went to court. Relieved and feeling more like himself . . .

B.J. Not guilty.

NEAL. Oh boy.

CLIFTON. Bert won *his* case. Sal Hepatica worked gently but thoroughly. Need a clever stocking stuffer? Try the new personalized plastic container of Sal Hepatica. Keep your whole family as regular as clockwork. But Sal Hepatica is only available in limited quantities to you because the country comes first. So, if Sal Hepatica is not on your druggist's shelf, please be patient, and know that the boys over there are getting the best.

[MUSIC NO. 6 "BLACK MAGIC"] (ANN *is waiting for* CANTONE *who is Off.*)

Ladies and gentlemen, Christmas time is always an extra special time for me because it was at Christmas time six years ago that I

started the Cavalcade. I found a singer who could warm even the
cockles of old Scrooge's heart. And she's still with us today.
Ladies and gents, New York's own, Ann Collier.

(*The "Applause" signs flash.* CANTONE *comes back Onstage
with a new drink, sets it on the piano, and walks* ANN *up to
the mic. They arrive, arguing. She kisses* CLIFTON. *During
"BLACK MAGIC"* CANTONE *sings into* CONNIE'S *ear. They
stand at the piano.* NEAL *watches* ANN *intently.*)

ANN. Thank you, Cliff. (*Sings.*)
THAT OLD BLACK MAGIC
HAS ME IN ITS SPELL
THAT OLD BLACK MAGIC
THAT YOU WEAVE SO WELL
THOSE ICY FINGERS
UP AND DOWN MY SPINE
THE SAME OLD WITCHCRAFT
WHEN YOUR EYES MEET MINE
THE SAME OLD TINGLE
THAT I FEEL INSIDE
AND THEN THAT ELEVATOR
STARTS ITS RIDE
AND DOWN AND DOWN I GO
ROUND AND ROUND I GO
LIKE A LEAF
THAT'S CAUGHT IN A TIDE
I SHOULD STAY AWAY
BUT WHAT CAN I DO
I HEAR YOUR NAME
AND I'M A FLAME
A FLAME WITH SUCH
A BURNING DESIRE
THAT ONLY YOUR KISS
CAN PUT OUT THE FIRE
SO YOU'RE THE LOVER
I HAVE WAITED FOR
THE MATE THAT FATE
HAD ME CREATED FOR
AND EVERY TIME YOUR LIPS MEET MINE
DARLING DOWN AND DOWN I GO
ROUND AND ROUND I GO
IN A SPIN

LOVING THE SPIN I'M IN
UNDER THAT OLD BLACK MAGIC CALLED LOVE
CALLED LOVE
CALLED LOVE
[MUSIC NO. 7 "AIN'T SHE SWEET"]

("Applause" signs flash. The Band plays the beginning to "AIN'T SHE SWEET." During the number, before the vocal, CONNIE *just leaves her chair with her Coke as* JOHNNY *beckons her over to where he's standing.* WALLY *thinks he's calling him and rushes over too.* JOHNNY *sends him back to his chair then puts his hand on* CONNIE's *shoulder which embarrasses her to death.* WALLY *is disillusioned.* B.J. *has just sat down in his chair.* WALLY *rats on* JOHNNY. B.J. *goes to get* CONNIE *away from* JOHNNY. *He does it pleasantly enough.* WALLY *is left looking at* JOHNNY *who glares at him.* B.J. *puts* CONNIE *in her chair.* WALLY *goes back over as* B.J. *and the Others [*GINGER, GENEVA *and* BIFF*] dance up to the center mic to sing the vocal.* B.J. *is still talking to* CONNIE. WALLY *comforts* CONNIE, *who pulls away and mouths "thanks a lot."* JOHNNY *has slithered into the greenroom to* ANN *who is sitting on* POPS' *desk. She greets him coolly. As the vocal begins,* CONNIE *stands up to go into the greenroom, sees* JOHNNY *with* ANN, *freezes a moment, then continues through to the anteroom.* JOHNNY *rolls his eyes then follows her in to apologize. You can see them arguing through the portal in the door.* NEAL *starts over to say something to* ANN—*something witty. Just as he leans in to her,* CLIFTON *comes over to ask her something.* NEAL *looks away embarrassed, and looks around to see if anyone saw him.* POPS *waves.* JOHNNY *comes out, followed by* CONNIE *still talking. She is still irritated and tries to get another Coke but is too agitated to hit the machine properly.* JOHNNY *gets it for her after placing his hand on hers. Suave. She melts.*)

ALL.
AIN'T SHE SWEET
SEE HER WALKIN' DOWN THE STREET
NOW I ASK YOU VERY CONFIDENTIALLY
AIN'T SHE SWEET
BIFF.
AIN'T SHE NICE
ALL.
MM-HMM

LOOK HER OVAH ONCE OR TWICE
NOW I ASK YOU VERY CONFIDENTIALLY
AIN'T SHE NICE
JUST CAST AN EYE
IN HER DI-RECTION
OH ME, OH MY
AIN'T SHE PERFECTION
SOLITUDEY, I
I REPEAT
THAT'S A GREAT SHAKE TRUCKIN' ON DOWN THE
    STREET
NOW I ASK YOU VERY CONFIDENTIALLY
AIN'T SHE SWEET—BOP BOP BOP

(Biff *plays "AIN'T SHE SWEET."*)

SEE HER WALKIN' DOWN THE STREET

(Biff *plays.*)

CAST AN EYE IN HER DIRECTION, PAPA, AN'
DIG THAT JIVE FROM FORE TO AFT
    B.J.
POPS, THAT'S PERFECTION
    Ginger.
SOLID
    Biff.
TAKE IT, BABY
    All.
SOLITUDEY
I REPEAT
THE CHICK IS MELLOW, OH OH
THE CHICK IS MEET
    Ginger.
DO YA DIG ME
    Geneva.
I MEAN
    Biff.
CONFIDENTIALLY
    All.
AIN'T SHE SWEET
            (*"Applause" signs flash.*)
    Clifton. That's Biff Baker and Boutinotes.
    Neal. Say, Cliff. The show's going great.

CLIFTON. Thanks Neal. You know, folks . . .
NEAL. I really love the way you do those ads.
CLIFTON. That's very kind of you, Neal. Folks . . .
NEAL. I really admire your style.
CLIFTON. Thanks, Neal, but we're on the air.
NEAL. I'm sorry I hate to interrupt.
CLIFTON. That's okay.
NEAL. I mean I know I don't like to get interrupted either.
CLIFTON. Right.
NEAL. So why should I interrupt you?
CLIFTON. That's the point.
NEAL. After all, we're on the air.
CLIFTON. Yes.
NEAL. So maybe it can wait til later.
CLIFTON. Thanks. Folks . . .
NEAL. But as long as I've got your ear.
CLIFTON. Neal, what is it?

(*During the following routine, the sound effects are done by* LOU *at the sound table.*)

NEAL. Can we step into your office for a second?
CLIFTON. What?
NEAL. It'll just take a second.
CLIFTON. Neal . . .
NEAL. Come on.

[MUSIC NO. 7A "COMEDY ROUTINE 1 & 2"]

(*Transition music plays. Door opens and shuts.*)
There that's better.
CLIFTON. Now what do you want, Neal?
NEAL. You need diction coaching.
CLIFTON. What?
NEAL. You need diction coaching.
CLIFTON. That's preposterous.
NEAL. You want to be like Gabriel Heater? You want to be like Walter Winchell?
CLIFTON. No.
NEAL. Then you need diction coaching. Now it just so happens that my diction teacher, Dr. Van Toyle, is in the neighborhood and said he'd give you a call.
(*Phone rings.*)
That's probably him. (*Answers phone.*) Dr. Van Toyle? He'd

love to work with you. (*Hangs up.*) He'll be right over.

(*Knocks.*)

Must have gotten tied up in traffic. (*Opens door.*) Dr. Van Toyle? Clifton Feddington. I'll just leave the two of you alone for a minute. Don't worry, Cliff, I'll take care of the show.

(*Door slams.*)

NEAL. (*Wearing a funny hat.*) Good evening, Mr. Feddington, nice to meet you. Just read this line please.

CLIFTON. This one? "Betty Botter baked a batch of buttered brownies."

NEAL. That's the line. Now try it.

CLIFTON. Betty Botter baked a batch—

NEAL. Just a minute, Mr. Feddington, please. Remember: in diction you must use ya woid which gives you da proper trelmedge in the mask area. Suppose you use a woid and people don't understand. You got gels with an equaline and vibins in your nose. Don't let that happen. Let your lips be felma. Try it again.

CLIFTON. Betty Botter—

NEAL. No no no, Mr. Feddington, *please.* Remember: in using the proper woid coming from the soft palette and svane, let the woid come out from da gorgle with lightness and dor*may.* You know you may have a sveenen da throat. You ribin teeth are getting in the way. After awl, you must realize what *is* diction but the woids coming out when a man is speaking forcefully and awgraing. Whether we speak or sing, no one can prodly do it without faffly knowing the correct do's and don'ts, dthees and dthaws. (*Ribbing him.*) Bedda men than you have equalined their time with the sedden ways that give them trouble. (*Laughs.*) Try it again.

CLIFTON. Betty Botter—

NEAL. Uh uh uh Mr. Feddington, please, we have to get it straight. Are you gonna dray back and forth? How do you fine the bradder placement? Naturally, we have to sfate the vowels. Et the thing you want it to draw. I had the same trouble with Victor Mature, but wid you, it's different. Try it again.

CLIFTON. Betty Botter—

NEAL. Mr. Feddington, Mr. Feddington!

CLIFTON. Yes?

NEAL. Why done you listen to the cray woids? You realize that any woid will give you crebits on the throat?

CLIFTON. I didn't know that.

NEAL. Just let the welman sound kline come out of the voice box.

CLIFTON. Oh I see.

NEAL. You do? Try it again.

CLIFTON. "Betty Botter drayed back and forth with lightness in the felma."

NEAL. Now you are getting it!

(*Music out.*)

CLIFTON. Neal Tilden, everyone!

(The Band starts playing the vamp intro to "HOW ABOUT YOU?" B.J. *helps* CONNIE *off with her jacket and runs a red comb through his hair once neatly, while* CLIFTON *introduce them.*)

Folks, you remember Bobby and Buddy Gibson on the Cavalcade from Christmases past. Well, this Christmas we've got their baby brother B.J. with us. B.J. Gibson, everyone.

[MUSIC NO. 8 "HOW ABOUT YOU"]

B.J.

WHEN A GIRL MEETS BOY
LIFE CAN BE A JOY
BUT THE NOTE THEY END ON
WILL DEPEND ON
LITTLE PLEASURES THEY WILL SHARE
SO LET US COMPARE

I LIKE NEW YORK IN JUNE
HOW ABOUT YOU
   CONNIE.
I LIKE A GERSHWIN TUNE
HOW ABOUT YOU
   B.J.
I LIKE A FIRESIDE
WHEN A STORM IS DUE
   BOTH.
I LIKE POTATO CHIPS
MOONLIGHT AND MOTOR TRIPS
HOW ABOUT YOU
   CONNIE.
I'M MAD ABOUT GOOD BOOKS
   B.J.
CAN'T GET MY FILL
AND FRANKLIN ROOSEVELT'S LOOKS
   CONNIE.
GIVE ME A THRILL

Both.
HOLDING HANDS IN THE MOVIE SHOW
WHEN ALL THE LIGHTS ARE LOW
MAY NOT BE NEW, BUT
I LIKE IT, HOW ABOUT YOU

(*Dance section. Soft shoe which* Lou *performs with sandpaper wood blocks and a pair of shoes. "Applause" signs flash after a particularly difficult section. The dance routine, no matter how good, is upstaged by a fire in the control booth.*)

Both. (*Continued.*)
I'D LOVE TO BRING ROMANCE
INTO YOUR LIFE
SO DARLING, WE SHOULD CHANCE
HUSBAND AND WIFE

WE COULD LIVE LIKE A MILLIONAIRE
NEVER A DOUBT OR CARE
THE PERFECT DU-O
Connie.
I LIKE IT, HOW ABOUT YOU
B.J.
I LIKE IT, HOW ABOUT YOU
Both.
WE LIKE IT, HOW ABOUT . . .
YOU!
(*"Applause" signs flash.*)

B.J. Clifton, could I just take a second to say hi to Bobby and Betty, who might be picking us up out at Eagle Pass Field, Eagle Pass, Texas. And to Buddy, who's overseas somewhere. This month he and Mimi are celebrating the one month old birthday of my little nephew, Bubba.

Clifton. Isn't *that* something? B.J. Gibson, everybody.

Ann. (*Quietly, sincerely.*) We were very gay the summer of '41. You took me somewhere almost every evening. Dancing, picnicking, swimming. Swimming I liked most of all. You called me a mermaid. A siren. A waterwitch. Then, on that never-to-be-forgotten afternoon at the beach . . . when I pulled off my swimcap . . . you told me that my hair was like a summer sunset shimmering on scarlet waves. That I'd bewitched you for keeps. You said, "Let's be sweethearts. For always." You're on the broad ocean now, Jim. You and millions of other Jims and Bills and Joes. But you'll be back. And know that I meant it when I said, "Yes. For always."

(*She walks quietly away from the mic.* CLIFTON *comes up to the center mic.*)

CLIFTON. The people who made those swimcaps are making lifesaving equipment today. Because we care about Jim too. The United States Rubber Company.

(ZOOT *begins vamp to "BLUE MOON."*)

Here's a song that's done quite a bit during its lifetime to further the sweet cause of romance. And we're seeing a new side of our comic, Neal Tilden. I'll bet you didn't know that Neal was a warm and sensitive balladeer. Neal Tilden, everyone.

(NEAL *is frantically looking at the sheet music. To get the last bit of confidence he needs to sing the song. He steps humbly to the microphone and speaks gently to the audience.*)

NEAL. I'd like to send this out to *Mrs.* Tilden if I may. (*Pause.*) Hi, Mom.

[MUSIC NO. 9 "BLUE MOON"]

(*He then sings "BLUE MOON." In the verse, however,* ZOOT *and the Drummer have pre-planned conspiracy. At the end of the first and second sentences, they hit Spike Jones-ish explosions of drums and piano.* CLIFTON *rushes over to* ZOOT *to see what happened and as* NEAL *has turned around to see too,* CLIFTON *urges him to continue.* NEAL *looks terribly hurt. Everyone is laughing Upstage of him. The Group [*WALLY, B.J., JOHNNY, ANN, GINGER *and* CONNIE*] are Center just by the piano.* CANTONE *conducts the Group with his cigarette and they sing "AMOS 'N' ANDY"-like choral work.* WALLY *is smelling* CONNIE'S *hair.*)

NEAL. (*Sings.*)
ONCE UPON A TIME, BEFORE I TOOK UP SMILING
I HATED THE MOONLIGHT (*Crash.*)
SHADOWS OF THE NIGHT THAT POETS FIND BEGUILING
SEEM FLAT AS THE NOON LIGHT (*Crash.*)
WITH NO ONE TO STAY UP FOR
I WENT TO SLEEP AT TEN
LIFE WAS A BITTER CUP FOR
THE SADDEST OF ALL MEN
BLUE MOON
YOU SAW ME STANDING ALONE

WITHOUT A DREAM IN MY HEART
WITHOUT A LOVE OF MY OWN
BLUE MOON
YOU KNEW JUST WHAT I WAS THERE FOR
YOU HEARD ME SAYING A PRAYER FOR
SOMEONE I REALLY COULD CARE FOR
AND THEN THERE SUDDENLY APPEARED BEFORE ME
THE ONLY ONE MY ARMS WOULD EVER HOLD
I HEARD SOMEBODY WHISPER PLEASE ADORE ME
AND WHEN I LOOKED THE MOON HAD TURNED TO
    GOLD

(LOU *turns the lights to gold.*)

BLUE MOON
NOW I'M NO LONGER ALONE
BLUE MOON
NOW I'M NO LONGER ALONE
WITHOUT A HEART
WITHOUT A LOVE OF MY OWN.

(NEAL, *at the end of the song, after totally screwing up the end of the song by beginning one phrase early, walks away from the mic like "So what? No big deal," but has forgotten dance routine he is supposed to do with* ANN. JOHNNY *prompts him to go back.* ANN *has already started.* CLIFTON *has sunk to one of the chairs and doesn't even watch. He and* ANN *dance. A complicated dance—a composite of tango, fox trot, ballroom—in which* ANN *does most of the dancing while* NEAL *first tries to catch up then "ad-libs" when his confidence is built enough. She continues to dance the dance as choreographed. With occasional moves which suggest there was supposed to be a partner. His trick pants fall down. He falls and otherwise ruins it. But thinks he's done beautifully.*)

ALL.
AH AH AH AH
AH AH AH AH
AH AH AH AH
    NEAL. (*Totally out of breath.*)
WITHOUT A LOVE OF MY OWN

(*"Applause" signs flash.* NEAL *bows several times. Looks at* CLIFTON *who is burning. The Band vamps into "CHIQUITA BANANA."*)

[MUSIC NO. 10 "CHIQUITA BANANA"]

ALL GIRLS.
I'M CHIQUITA BANANA AND I COME TO SAY
I COME FROM LEETLE ISLAND DOWN EQUATOR WAY
I SAIL ON BEEG BANANA BOT FROM
CARIBEE, TO SEE IF I CAN HELP
GOOD NEIGHBOR POLICY
I SING A SONG ABOUT BANANAS
I SING IT LOW, I SING IT HI-EEEEEE
I MAKE BEEG HIT WITH MERICANOS
SINGING SONG ABOUT BANANOS
I COULD SING ABOUT THE MOONLIGHT
ON THE VERY, VERY TROPICAL EQUATOR
BUT NO I SING ABOUT BANANAS
AND THE REFRIGERATOR—SI, SI, SI, SI!

(*NOTE: Productions which cut the character of* GENEVA *should also cut the following number: Band begins "ROSE OF THE RIO GRANDE."*)

[MUSIC NO. 11 "ROSE OF THE RIO GRANDE"]

CLIFTON. (*Over the Band.*) And now, straight from standing room only engagements at Chicago's Rhumboogie Club, Kyle's Place in Nashville, Virginia's in Los Angeles, the Chesterfield Club in Kansas City, and New York's own Onyx Club on 52nd Street, featuring members of her combo, the Kansas City Brown Boys, ladies and gentlemen, Geneva Lee Browne.
GENEVA.
ROSE OF THE RIO GRANDE
ROSE OF THE BORDERLAND
ONE WORD AND HAND IN HAND
WE'LL LEAVE THE PREACHER'S SIDE ROOM
HAPPY LITTLE BRIDE AND BRIDEGROOM
OVER THOSE HILLS OF SAND
I'VE GOT OUR LOVE NEST PLANNED
YOU NAME IT
I'LL CLAIM IT
ROSE OF RIO GRANDE
MEN & BAND. (GENEVA *scats or dances.*)
ROSA
ROSE
ROSA YOU'RE A DARLIN

ROSA
ROSE
A LIVIN DOLL
WOO HOO
THAT'S SOME ROSA
ROSE
ROSE
OF THE RIO GRANDE
ROSA
ROSE
OF THE BORDER LAND
                    (*Wolf whistle.*)
THAT'S MY ROSA
                    (*Band and scat break.*)
    MEN. (B.J. *and* NEAL *showing* WALLY *what to do.*)
ROSE OF THE RIO GRANDE
ROSE OF THE BORDER LAND

ROSA
ROSA
ROSA
    GENEVA & MEN.
ROSA OF THE RIO GRANDE!

(*The "Applause" signs flash.* ZOOT *begins the Johnny Theme.*
    JOHNNY *is coming up to the mic this time with a cigarette
    and his drink. He wears his hat back on his head.*)

    CLIFTON. Geneva Lee Browne!! Ladies and gentlemen, it's
time again for "The Cantone tone." Our featured vocalist
tonight, Johnny Cantone. Johnny?

(*The "Applause" signs flash.* JOHNNY *comes up to the mic with
    his manhattan in plain sight.* CLIFTON *glances at it.*)

    JOHNNY. Thank you . . . thank you . . . You know, Cliff, a
good buddy of mine, Frankie Sinatra is gonna be playing the
Paramount with Benny Goodman next week.
                    (*"Applause" signs flash. He nods.*)
Thank you, yeah, we're both pretty pleased about it. Well,
Frankie passed along a new arrangement to me and I wonder if I
might give it a shot?
    CLIFTON. (*Grabbing the drink out of* JOHNNY'S *hand.*) You got
it, Johnny.

    [MUSIC NO. 12 "I'LL NEVER SMILE AGAIN"]

(JOHNNY, *tipsy, hardly sings but lets the Quintet carry it.*)

QUINTET. (NEAL, B.J., ANN, GINGER, CONNIE.)
I'LL NEVER SMILE AGAIN
UNTIL I SMILE AT YOU
I'LL NEVER SMILE AGAIN
JOHNNY.
WHAT GOOD WOULD IT DO?
FOR TEARS WOULD FILL MY EYES
MY HEART WOULD REALIZE
QUINTET.
THAT OUR ROMANCE IS THROUGH
I'LL NEVER LOVE AGAIN
I'M SO IN LOVE WITH YOU
I'LL NEVER THRILL AGAIN
JOHNNY.
TO SOMEBODY NEW
WITHIN MY HEART
I KNOW I COULD NEVER START
QUINTET.
TO SMILE AGAIN
JOHNNY.
UNTIL I SMILE AT YOU
(*Instrumental break.* JOHNNY *smells his flower. During instrumental break, spoken.*)
Fritz Canigliaro on trombone. Ah, play it pretty. (*Singing.*)
WITHIN MY HEART
I KNOW I COULD NEVER START
ALL.
TO SMILE AGAIN
JOHNNY.
UNTIL I SMILE AT YOU
          (*Instrumental break.* JOHNNY *removes his flower.*)
UNTIL I
ALL.
SMILE AT YOU

(JOHNNY *tosses his flower into the audience. And puts out his cigarette on the floor.* CLIFTON *comes forward. "Applause" signs flash.* CLIFTON *points to cigarette butt on floor and* LOU *picks it up.*)

CLIFTON. You know, folks, we'd like to take this time to wish each and every one of you a Merry Christmas and thank you for tuning in on this snowy New York Evening. And while we're on the subject of Christmas, let's not forget about iced cream. No no. Before that holly-decked clock strikes another chime, rest an Eskimo Pie between your lips.

(GINGER *steps up to the mic, removes her gum.*)

GINGER. (*Suggestively.*) Send your teeth exploring through that crisp robe of fine, pure chocolate. Down . . . down . . . down . . . into that creamy center of wholesome delicious iced cream.
(CLIFTON *is lost. He doesn't seem to have this part in his script.*)
Close your eyes and let those two tempting treats melt . . . melt . . . melt in your mouth and blend into a symphony of flavor.
(CLIFTON *thinks it's over. It's not.*)
Mmmmmmmmmmmmmmmmmmmmmmm. You've discovered somethin'.

(CLIFTON *and* LOU *and just about Everyone Else are stunned.* GINGER *puts her gum back in her mouth and smiles as she backs away from the mic, waving.*)

CLIFTON. Eskimo Pie. At leading Drug Stores and confectionaries everywhere.
(*The Drummer starts a quick high hat beat.*)
[MUSIC NO. 13 "BOOGIE WOOGIE BUGLE BOY"]
You know folks, we've got a special treat for you tonight. It's taken us almost a year to get this famously famous trio of gals back together again. They've been stolen away from us by the War, the movies and whatnot. This is the first time that Geneva Lee Browne has ever seen this chart, got a little backed up in rehearsal time, but she's such a trooper, she's gonna do it cold.

(*Trumpet solo starts.*)

GENEVA. Honey, I don't do nothin' cold.

(*She laughs as she walks Off,* LOU *chasing after her.* CLIFTON *grabs the music away from her and grabs* B.J. *out of his chair to join* GINGER *and* CONNIE *just in time. They sing:* B.J. *reads [sings] from sheet music.*)

B.J., CONNIE, GINGER.
HE WAS A FAMOUS TRUMPET MAN FROM OUT

CHICAGO WAY
HE HAD A BOOGIE SOUND THAT NO ONE ELSE COULD
  PLAY
HE WAS THE TOP MAN AT HIS CRAFT
BUT THEN HIS NUMBER CAME UP
AND HE WAS CAUGHT IN THE DRAFT
HE'S IN THE ARMY NOW, A-BLOWIN REVEILLE
HE'S THE BOOGIE WOOGIE BUGLE BOY OF COMPANY B
THEY MADE HIM BLOW A BUGLE FOR HIS UNCLE SAM
IT REALLY BROUGHT HIM DOWN BECAUSE HE COULD
  NOT JAM
THE CAPTAIN SEEMED TO UNDERSTAND
BECAUSE THE NEXT DAY THE CAP
WENT OUT AND DRAFTED A BAND
AND NOW THE COMPANY JUMPS
WHEN HE PLAYS REVEILLE
HE'S THE BOOGIE WOOGIE BUGLE BOY OF COMPANY B
A ROOT A TOOT TOOTLE EE AH DA TOOT
HE BLOWS EIGHT TO THE BAR
IN BOOGIE RHYTHM
HE CAN'T BLOW A NOTE UNLESS A BASS 'N' GUITAR
'Z' PLAYIN' WITH 'IM
AND THE COMPANY JUMPS WHEN HE PLAYS REVEILLE
HE'S THE BOOGIE WOOGIE BUGLE BOY OF COMPANY B!

(*Instrumental break.* GENEVA *re-enters with* CLIFTON. *They are
   yelling at each other—still arguing over the incident. She
   hears* B.J. *singing then* CLIFTON *hears him singing. And they
   both laugh.*)

HE PUTS THE BOYS TO SLEEP WITH BOOGIE EVERY
  NIGHT
AND WAKES EM UP THE SAME WAY IN THE EARLY
  BRIGHT
THEY CLAP THEIR HANDS AND STAMP THEIR FEET
FOR THEY KNOW HOW HE BLOWS WHEN SOMEONE
  GIVE HIM A BEAT
HE REALLY BREAKS IT UP WHEN HE PLAYS REVEILLE
HE'S THE BOOGIE WOOGIE BUGLE BOY OF COMPANY B
                (B.J. *throws aside music.*)
BOP BAH BOP DOO WAH
BOP BAH BOP DOO WAH

BOP BAH BOP DOO WAH
BOP BAH BOP DOO WAH
AND THE COMPANY JUMPS
WHEN HE PLAYS REVEILLE
HE'S THE BOOGIE WOOGIE BUGLE BOY OF COMPANY B

(*"Applause" signs flash.*)

CLIFTON. That's one of the finest singing trios of gals we've ever had on WOV! (*Suddenly urgent, reading from a telegram.*) Bulletin. Bulletin. Bulletin.
(*The Cast is alert.*)
Gingivitis attacking thousands throughout the nation. You say you haven't got Gingivitis. Well, don't be too sure. Gingivitis is so common today that four out of five men, women and even children have this horrible gum infection often a forerunner to disgusting pyorrhea. One warning sign is tender, bleeding gums, you might check. Come on, do the tongue test with me right now. Run the tip of your tongue throughout the inside of your mouth. (WALLY, *standing, and* GINGER, *at her seat, do the tongue test as* CLIFTON *suggests.*)
Did your gums feel sore? If they did, you have Gingivitis. (*Realizing that he's left out a possibility. Ad libs to cover. Not too well.*) If they didn't, you still could be getting Gingivitis, so one way or the other, it's time you switched to Forhan's. The original anti-Gingivitis formula that works fast at removing that acid film that causes tooth decay and bleeding gums. Remember, that's Forhan's. (*Spelling.*) F-O-R (*Pause.*) H-A-N.
NEAL. (*Quietly. Off mic.*) S.
CLIFTON. (*After a brief look at* NEAL.) S. And now . . .
(*Fanfare.*) [MUSIC NO. 14 "SERVEL ELECTROLUX"]
The Servel Electrolux Refrigerator Giveaway!
(*Music theme.*)
Each week we award a beautiful new Servel Refrigerator—the only refrigerator with no moving parts— to the first of our listeners who calls in and in twenty-five words or less completes the phrase, "I like Servel Refrigerators because . . ."
CONNIE. Oh, Clifton, I'm so excited.
CLIFTON. Say, cute little Connie Miller, how would *you* complete that phrase? "I like Servel Refrigerator because..."
(*Drum roll.*)
CONNIE. (*Really caught unawares.*) Well, I like Servel

Refrigerators because . . . they work so good.

CLIFTON. (*Music theme and applause.*) Hey! A great answer, Connie! Now all you listeners out there, no fair stealing Connie's answer. You've gotta come up with one of your own. Now you have sixty seconds to call WOV to claim your prize. So get on your telephone and call WOV at Circle 5-7979, that's Circle 5-7979. Operators are standing by.

(POPS *steps forward to phone. He's wearing his holey sweater and self-conscious about his appearance.*)

You have sixty seconds from . . . now.

(*Everyone tenses. The Band is playing the "Mutual Manhattan Variety Cavalcade" version of ticking music.* LOU *watches the stop watch.* CONNIE *bounces a little on her toes.* NEAL *smokes his pipe resolutely. The Band has played the phrase six times. No one calls. Everyone shifts weight at the same time. All are staring at the phone.*)

CLIFTON. (*Softly.*) Lines are still open.

(*Silence. The phone rings.* POPS *answers.*)

POPS. WOV Servel Refrigerator Giveaway Contest. (*Pause.*) Uh huh. Uh huh.

(*Nods to* CLIFTON. CLIFTON *beams.* POPS *gets out his pencil and pad.*)

Yeah. Bashful Daddy in the first race—

CLIFTON. (*Cutting it off.*) Wrong number!

(POPS *continues his conversation.* LOU *is trying to take phone away from him. Music theme and out.*)

Ha ha ha ha. How about that.

POPS. (*To* LOU, *off-mic.*) How the hell was I supposed to . . .

CLIFTON. (*Covering.*) Oh boy. Ha ha ha ha. Ginger Brooks, everyone.

GINGER. (*Stepping up to the mic. The Four Men are at the left mic, facing forward. Very macho.* WALLY *shines his shoes on the back of his pants.*) I love contests.

(CLIFTON, LOU *and* POPS *are arguing off-mic.*)

I'd like to send this song out to my mother. Who taught me all the lessons I had to go out and learn myself. Ready boys?

(ZOOT *gives her a note.*)

Thank you Zoot.

(ZOOT *gives her the note again.* LOU *is a little impatient. He looks at* CLIFTON. *Proud already of the number. He's a little worried about* WALLY. *She sings "BLUES IN THE NIGHT.")*

[MUSIC NO. 15 "BLUES IN THE NIGHT"]

MY MAMA DONE TOLD ME

MEN.

HUNH!

GINGER.

WHEN I WAS IN PIGTAILS

MEN.

HUNH!

GINGER.

MY MAMA DONE TOLE ME, HON

MEN.

HOO WEE

GINGER.

A MAN'S GONNA SWEET TALK
AND GIVE YA THE BIG EYE
BUT WHEN THAT SWEET TALKIN'S DONE
A MAN IS A TWO FACE
A WORRISOME THING
WHO'LL LEAVE YOU TO SING
THE BLUES IN THE NIGHT
NOW THE RAIN'S A FALLIN'
HEAR THE TRAIN A CALLIN'

MEN.

HOO WEE

GINGER.

MY MAMA DONE TOLE ME
HEAR THAT LONESOME WHISTLE
BLOWIN' CROSS THE TRESTLE

MEN.

HOO WEE

GINGER.

MY MAMA DONE TOLE ME

MEN.

A HOO WEE DA HOO WEE, AW
CLICKETY CLACK

GINGER.

ECHOING BACK
THE BLUES IN THE NIGHT
FROM NATCHEZ TO MOBILE

FROM MEMPHIS TO SAINT JOE
WHEREVER THE FOUR WINDS BLOW
I BEEN IN SOME BIG TOWNS
AND I HEARD ME SOME BIG TALK
BUT THERE IS ONE THING I KNOW
A MAN IS A TWO FACE
A WORRISOME THING
WHO'LL LEAVE YOU TO SING
THE BLUES IN THE NIGHT
IN THE NIGHT . . . IN THE NIGHT

(*R-rated dance routine.* CLIFTON *is stunned.* LOU *moves with his choreography.* WALLY *screws up.*)

MEN.

HOOOOO WEEEEE
HOOOOO WEEEEE

GINGER.

MY MAMA WAS RIGHT.
THERE'S BLUES IN THE NIGHT.

(*"Applause" signs flash.* WALLY *helps a pretty drunk* CANTONE *to his feet.* CANTONE *goes Offstage. Band vamps into:*

[MUSIC NO. 16 "JINGLE BELLS"]

CONNIE & GINGER.

TIS THE SEASON OF CHRISTMAS AND ALL THRU THE
BAND

B.J., ANN, WALLY.

WE'RE SWINGIN' AND RINGIN' AND ROCKIN' THE
STAND

ALL.

THE TRUMPETS ARE BLARIN' AND BURSTIN' WITH
PRIDE

ANN.

AND THE SAXES AND BONES MAKE US SATISFIED,
NOW I'M SPEAKIN' FOR CLIFTON AND THE FIVE BOU-
TINIERES,

B.J.

IT'S TIME TO FORGET ALL YOUR WORRIES AND FEARS

CONNIE.

SO FOR ZOOT AND FOR BIFF AND IN FACT THE WHOLE
BAND

ALL.

FROM US MERRY CHRISTMAS TO ALL THE LAND

(*Instrumental break. Then* BIFF *sings.*)

BIFF.
DASHING THRU THE SNOW
IN A ONE HORSE OPEN SLEIGH
O'ER THE FIELDS WE GO
LAUGHING ALL THE WAY

(*Cast laughs.*)

BELLS ON BOBTAILS RING
MAKING SPIRITS BRIGHT
WHAT FUN IT IS TO RIDE AND SING
A SLEIGHING SONG TONIGHT
GROUP.
JINGLE BELLS, JINGLE BELLS
BIFF.
JINGLE ALL THE WAY
OH WHAT FUN IT IS TO RIDE
IN A ONE HORSE OPEN SLEIGH
GROUP.
JINGLE BELLS, JINGLE BELLS
BIFF.
I DON'T MIND THE STORM
GRAB YOUR COATS AND HATS, YOU LUKEWARM CATS
I GOT MY HORN TO KEEP ME WARM

(*Band goes to rhumba.* NEAL *enters wearing a sombrero, pretending to ride a horse. He sings:*)

NEAL.
DOWN IN MEXICO
WE AIN'T GOT NO SNOW
GROUP.
YOU AIN'T GOT NO SNOW?
NEAL.
NO, NO, NO
DOWN IN MEXICO
SIT AROUND ALL DAY
HEAR DE MUSIC PLAY
EVERYTIME WE SING
TEQUILA GLASSES RING

(*The Band clinks glasses with spoons.*)

GROUP.
JINGLE, JINGLE, JINGLE, JINGLE

(BIFF *plays a solo. Big instrumental ending. "Applause" signs flash.*)

CLIFTON. That's Biff Baker and the Boutinaturals, everyone. Biff, that was just swell, but what's this I hear about your leaving us?

BIFF. That's right, Clifton. It's been great to be back, even if only for a week. I really love being around you guys. As many of you know, I've been in flight training now for about six months and tomorrow I'm going overseas to join a fighter squadron. Can't say where I'm going. Uh . . . Clifton, could I just take another second?

(CLIFTON *smiles and nods, waves* LOU *away.*)
I got a call tonight from my folks in Greenwood, Indiana, and they said the best Christmas present I could give them next year would be my being home. And I'd like to say that I think we can do it. If we all work together. All of you here and all of us guys overseas. And keep other guys from having to get involved in this thing. So let's all work hard and get this over by Christmas of 1943.

[MUSIC NO. 17 "I GOT IT BAD"]

(*"Applause" signs flash.* CANTONE *comes back Onstage from Left hallway with a new drink. He leans up against* CLIFTON'S *office door. Piano vamps.* CANTONE *and* CLIFTON *smoke.* BIFF *sits on the riser near the piano. It's the atmosphere of a club late at night.* GENEVA *sings:*)

(*NOTE: In productions which cut the character of* GENEVA, *this song should be sung by* ANN.)

GENEVA.
THE POETS SAY THAT ALL WHO LOVE ARE BLIND
BUT I'M IN LOVE AND I KNOW WHAT TIME IT IS
THE GOOD BOOK SAYS "GO SEEK AND YE SHALL FIND,"
WELL, I HAVE SOUGHT AND MY WHAT A CLIMB IT IS
MY LIFE IS JUST LIKE THE WEATHER
IT CHANGES WITH THE HOURS
WHEN HE'S NEAR I'M FAIR AND WARMER

WHEN HE'S GONE I'M CLOUDY WITH SHOWERS
IN EMOTION, LIKE THE OCEAN
IT'S EITHER SINK OR SWIM
WHEN A WOMAN LOVES A MAN LIKE I LOVE HIM
NEVER TREATS ME SWEET AND GENTLE
THE WAY HE SHOULD—I GOT IT BAD
AND THAT AIN'T GOOD
MY POOR HEART IS SENTIMENTAL
NOT MADE OF WOOD—I GOT IT BAD
AND THAT AIN'T GOOD
BUT WHEN THE WEEKEND'S OVER
AND MONDAY ROLLS AROUND
I END UP LIKE I START OUT
CRYIN' MY HEART OUT
HE DON'T LOVE ME LIKE I LOVE HIM
NOBODY COULD
I GOT IT BAD AND THAT AIN'T GOOD

(*Instrumental.*)

I GOT IT BAD, SO BAD, SO BAD
THE FOLKS WITH GOOD INTENTIONS
TELL ME TO SAVE MY TEARS
I'M GLAD I'M MAD ABOUT HIM
I JUST CAN'T LIVE WITHOUT HIM
LORD ABOVE ME, MAKE HIM LOVE ME
THE WAY HE SHOULD; I GOT IT BAD
AND THAT AIN'T GOOD, THAT AIN'T GOOD
LIKE A LONELY WEEPING WILLOW LOST IN THE
  WOOD
THE THINGS I TELL MY PILLOW, NO WOMAN SHOULD
I GOT IT BAD, BAD; SO BAD
AND THAT AIN'T GOOD.

(*"Applause" signs flash. Piano vamps* JOHNNY'S *theme.*)

CLIFTON. (*Reverent.*) Ladies and gentlemen. Our featured vocalist tonight.

(LOU *is grabbing at* CLIFTON'S *coat,* CLIFTON *waves him off.*) And every night. Johnny Cantone. Johnny?

(CLIFTON *turns and* JOHNNY'S *not there.* LOU *has the "I tried to*

tell you" look on his face and gestures down the hall. CLIF-
TON *runs Off down the hall.* ZOOT *is still playing.* JOHNNY
comes On ahead of CLIFTON *keeping his drink about a foot
away from* CLIFTON'S *hand. Some People roll their eyes.
Some of the Musicians laugh. You get the impression that
this has happened many times, especially of late, and that
it's all part of* JOHNNY. JOHNNY *arrives at the mic, looking a
little disheveled. Smiles at the audience. He takes a drink.
He looks a little puzzled and looks back to the Band.)*

JOHNNY. Who are all these people and what do they want here?
(CLIFTON *whispers to* JOHNNY.)
Okay, Zoot, let's get it over with.

(The Band plays a big deal intro to "YOU GO TO MY HEAD."
JOHNNY'S *weaving a little bit. There is a pause for the vocal to
begin.* JOHNNY *doesn't sing, but takes a drink.* CLIFTON *pleads.*
JOHNNY *laughs.* CLIFTON *threatens him.* ZOOT *plays again.*
JOHNNY'S *theme on the piano.)*

Hold it, Zoot, hold it.
(Everyone freezes. This has never happened. LOU *is still timing,
making notes on his clip board and shuffling through pages
of script to see what can be cut.* JOHNNY *hikes up his pants.)*
Ladies and gentlemen, you've heard enough of me over the
years, these past few years. I been kicking around here with Zoot
and Cliff and the band just about six years now. *(He laughs.)* In
1936, Clifton went to my uncle with this idea for a show. My uncle said sure. I got this nephew, Johnny. Just got married.
Wants to be a singer. Got a good voice.
(*Pause.* CLIFTON *needs his Bromo.)*
I gotta get outta here. *(He laughs but it stops short and he thinks
about something.)* Anyway, this is my last night playing this
hall.
(Everyone looks at each other. No one knew. NEAL *knew. And
starts to wise up.* CLIFTON *gets a call and takes it on* POPS'
desk phone. It's Saul Lebowitz and one can tell by the way
CLIFTON *can't get a word in that he's not too happy.)*
I'm going out to Hollywood. To make some movies. And some
money. And maybe even to see my wife. Clifton knows all about
this.
*(He doesn't. Everyone looks at him. He shrugs his shoulders
wildly then looks embarrassed at the audience and slips his*

hand in his pocket nonchalantly.)

I'd like to introduce you to the kid I've chosen to take my place here as "featured vocalist" with Zoot and the boys.

(CLIFTON *sees* NEAL *approaching the spotlight and drops the phone.* POPS *hangs it up after softly saying "Good bye."* NEAL *looks at him like "That's the breaks."* CLIFTON *puts his hands on his head and walks away toward* LOU.)

He's a fine guy. He hasn't been here too long but it's been long enough to make a real impression on me. You know his work. He's a fine singer. Dancer too.

(NEAL *is embarrassed by all the praise.* JOHNNY *is leaning on* NEAL'S *shoulder for support.*)

He's gonna be surprised, I think. Well, you know who I mean. And I think it's time you heard him. Ladies and Gentlemen, B.J. Gibson.

(B.J. *is in shock. So is* NEAL *who is frozen in mid-gesture of acceptance.* B.J. *steps forward.* NEAL *stands next to him for a moment.*)

You know this tune, don't you, B.J.?

    B.J. I think so.

    JOHNNY. Then sing it for us.

(LOU *has brought the music up to give to* B.J. NEAL *takes it and gives it to him then shakes his hand and walks away defeated and conned.* JOHNNY *walks over to the greenroom and sits on the step.* WALLY *watches him.* ANN *does too.* POPS *watches* ANN. B.J. *looks over the music while the Band intros "YOU GO TO MY HEAD."* B.J. *sings.*)

[MUSIC NO. 18 "YOU GO TO MY HEAD"]

    B.J.

YOU GO TO MY HEAD
AND YOU LINGER LIKE A HAUNTING REFRAIN
AND I FIND YOU SPINNING 'ROUND IN MY BRAIN
LIKE THE BUBBLES IN A GLASS OF CHAMPAGNE.

YOU GO TO MY HEAD
LIKE A SIP OF SPARKLING BURGUNDY BREW
AND I FIND THE VERY MENTION OF YOU
LIKE THE KICKER IN A JULEP OR TWO.

THE THRILL OF THE THOUGHT
THAT YOU MIGHT GIVE A THOUGHT TO MY PLEA

CASTS A SPELL OVER ME.
STILL I SAY TO MYSELF,
"GET AHOLD OF YOURSELF,
CAN'T YOU SEE THAT IT NEVER CAN BE."

YOU GO TO MY HEAD
WITH A SMILE THAT MAKES MY TEMP'RATURE RISE,
LIKE A SUMMER WITH A THOUSAND JULYS,
YOU INTOXICATE MY SOUL WITH YOUR EYES.

THO I'M CERTAIN THAT THIS HEART OF MINE
HASN'T A GHOST OF A CHANCE IN THIS CRAZY
    ROMANCE,
YOU GO TO MY HEAD.
YOU GO TO MY HEAD.

    (*Alto solo, followed by full orchestra instrumental.*)
    B.J.
YOU GO TO MY HEAD
WITH A SMILE THAT MAKES MY TEMP'RATURE RISE,
LIKE A SUMMER WITH A THOUSAND JULYS,
YOU INTOXICATE MY SOUL WITH YOUR EYES.

THO I'M CERTAIN THAT THIS HEART OF MINE
HASN'T A GHOST OF A CHANCE IN THIS CRAZY
    ROMANCE,
YOU GO TO MY HEAD.
YOU GO TO MY HEAD.

    (*"Applause" signs flash.*)

[MUSIC NO. 19 "FIVE O'CLOCK WHISTLE"]

    CLIFTON. B.J. Gibson, everyone.
(*The Band goes right into "THE FIVE O'CLOCK WHISTLE."*
    CONNIE *steps up and sings:*)
    CONNIE.
THE FIVE O'CLOCK WHISTLE'S ON THE BLINK.
THE WHISTLE WON'T BLOW AND WHADD'YA THINK?
MY POP IS STILL IN THE FACTORY
'CAUSE HE DON'T KNOW WHAT TIME IT HAPPENS
    TO BE.

THE FIVE O'CLOCK WHISTLE DIDN'T BLOW;

THE WHISTLE IS BROKE AND WHADDAYA KNOW?
IF SOMEBODY DON'T FIND OUT WHAT'S WRONG,
OH MY POP'LL BE WORKING ALL NIGHT LONG.
   BAND.
OH! WHO'S GONNA FIX THE WHISTLE?
WON'T SOMEBODY FIX THE WHISTLE?
WHO'S GONNA FIX THE WHISTLE?
   CONNIE.
SO MY POOR OLD POP WILL KNOW IT'S TIME FOR HIM
   TO STOP.
YOU OUGHTA HEAR WHAT MY MOMMY SAID,
WHEN PAPA CAME HOME AND SNEAKED INTO BED,
AND TOLD HER HE WORKED TILL HALF-PAST TWO
'CAUSE THE FIVE O'CLOCK WHISTLE NEVER BLEW.

(The Band breaks into an uptempo instrumental. Eventually, after much badgering and out of random dancing around, CONNIE and B.J. are persuaded, NEAL and GINGER too, to jitterbug to the rest of the number. After a short while, it is clear who the experts are, and the others stop dancing and as CONNIE and B.J. dance, the others watch and shout at them. JOHNNY comes out wearing the sombrero. CLIFTON is at the center mic. Big lights shift. Light coming up on CLIFTON'S chin. During the following section, LOU again does the sound effects.)

And now . . .
(Organ chord. ZOOT plays from the booth—Orson Welles style.)
. . . Mysterious Curtains.
     (Build. Gunshot. GINGER screams. Chord.)
Yes, Mysterious Curtains. WOV's weekly excursion into the unknown. Tonight, the Feddington Players present . . .
     (Cheery piano "DECK THE HALLS.")
our traditional radio adaptation of Dickins' immortal Yuletide classic, A Christmas Carol, featuring Neal Tilden, brought to you by Nash, the car that's built like a bridge, Nash is here to stay.
(POPS tunes his radio more closely and listens intently to the drama as it proceeds.)
Imagine if you will, London

     [MUSIC NO. 20 "MYSTERIOUS CURTAINS CUE NO. 1]

     (Big Ben chimes in the Orchestra.)
of more than a hundred years ago . . .

GENEVA. Christmas cakes, fresh tasty bread . . .

B.J. Chimney sweep, chimney sweep . . .

CLIFTON. It's Christmas time.

(*Sleigh bells.*)

The snow is falling gently on the town.

(*Dog bark.*)

The jingle of sleighbells . . .

(*Bells.*)

And the clip-clop of carriages . . .

(*Hooves, carriage. Carrollers sing "DECK THE HALLS" and continue through the following lines.*)

Carrollers, children playing around the bonfire.

CONNIE. Get away from me, Tommy, get away.

B.J. Hide and seek. Hide and seek.

CONNIE. Where are you. (*She giggles.*)

(*In this section, the Performers drop loose sheets of script onto the floor silently as they finish with them.*)

CLIFTON. Then there was Scrooge.

(*"DECK THE HALLS" stops.*)

NEAL. Bah! Humbug!

CLIFTON. I remember old Ebenezer Scrooge shutting up his counting house that Christmas Eve.

(*Door locks.*)

Setting out for his own home where he looked forward to spending a nice quiet night alone.

NEAL. This blizzard. I'll never get home.

[MYSTERIOUS CURTAINS CUE NO. 2]

(*Band Plays a real shaky "GOD REST YE."*)

Oh, no! That wretched tune again. Get back to your homes, you're creating a nuisance!

(*Band stops. Slight deflating bagpipes.*)

B.J. Tuppence for the poor, guv'na?

NEAL. I'll give you tuppence. Take that! (*Striking sound.*)

B.J. Aw! (*Falling sound.*) Ohhhhhhhh.

NEAL. I'll just turn down this alley.

(*Snow walking. Plunger wind.*)

Mmmmm. The snow is deeper than I thought.

(*Wind.*)

JOHNNY. Scrooge . . . (*Wind and walking out.*)

NEAL. Who is it? Where are you?
> (*Fast snow walking.* NEAL *breathes heavily.*)

Ah, home at last.

CLIFTON. Scrooge arrived home and climbed the many flights of rickety steps (*Door.*) to his garret flat.

NEAL. Mmmm . . . cold.
> (*Hand warming. Stairs. Keys. Door. Step in. Door.*)

One more flight.

(*Everyone looks around.* NEAL *is padding his part.* LOU *does stairs #2. Keys. Door. Step in. Door.*)

CLIFTON. Scrooge locked himself up tight.
> (*Door locks.*)

When suddenly at the window . . .
> (*Window breaks. Everyone moans like phantoms.*)

The air was filled with phantoms all moaning in chains. The clock struck one.

(LOU *has entrusted one sound effect with* WALLY, *who mistakenly hits a pan lid. Everyone looks around at the "thwack."* LOU *takes the mallet from* WALLY *and hits the correct chime.*)

Scrooge leapt into his bed.
> (*Pillow.*)

And hid under the covers.
> (*Covers. Knocks on door.*)

NEAL. Go away from my door. I won't let you in.
> (*Knocking.*)

GENEVA. (*Wearing thick glasses.*) I'm already in, honey.

(*Chime.* CLIFTON *glares at* GENEVA.)

NEAL. Who and what are you?

GENEVA. I am the Ghost of Christmas Past. Rise and walk with me.

NEAL. Why?

GENEVA. I will show you.

NEAL. What?

GENEVA. Yourself.
> (*Chimes.*)

CLIFTON. They passed through the wall. And suddenly they found themselves on a country road.
> (*Bells.*)

with fields on either side.
                    (*Dog barks.*)
It was a crisp, quilt-cold winter's day.
    NEAL. I was born in this place. I was a boy here.
        (*Children singing "LONDON BRIDGE" softly.*)
There's Bobby, Dick, Mary and Tom. It is I, Ebenezer.
    GENEVA. These are but shadows of things that have been. They
have no consciousness of us.
    NEAL. Wait. That's me. Alone. I was always left alone.
Holidays and all. Oh, Spirit, take me back.
                    (*Phantoms start.*)
I cannot bear to see any more. Take me back, please. Please.
Please. Please.
            (*Cut off. Wrestling in the bed.*)
Please. Please. Please.
                    (*Ticking.*)
I'm in my bed. Have I been dreaming?
                    (*Cautiously.*)
Spirit?
                    (*Quietly.*)
An illusion. A nightmare. Heh heh heh.
                (*Fluffing pillow.*)
Time for bed. Imagine. Spirits. (*He snores.*)
                    (*Knocking.*)
What was that?
    B.J. (*Into cup.*) Ebenezer Scrooge?
    NEAL. Nobody's here.
    B.J. Ebenezer Scrooge?
    NEAL. He's been called away.
    B.J. Ho ho ho ho . . .
    NEAL. Get away from my door.
            (*Pounding. Spelling it out. A cue.*)
No. You are breaking down my door!
        (*Door breaking down. Pounding. Phantoms.*)
No. No. No. No.
(*Cut off. Instant cheery piano music: "DECK THE HALLS."*)
    CLIFTON. (*Quickly.*) Return with us next week for the conclu-
sion of Charles Dickens' "A Christmas Carol" brought to you
by Nash.
(*"Applause" signs flash.* CLIFTON *is at the center mic.* LOU
    performs marching men.)

Marching ahead full speed on national defense. Ten acres of floor space. Three shifts a day. Two hundred twenty-three sub-contractors supplying machines and material to build a new type of heavy machine gun which naval authorities describe as the most effective weapon of its size ever produced.

(*The Soldiers stop marching.*)

Nash. We build the perfect car for America. And now a new weapon to win the War. National defense. First. At Nash.

[MUSIC NO. 21 "W.O.U. STATION NO. 1"]

GROUP. (*At center mic. They sing.*) WOV.

CLIFTON. WOV for Victory time is nine.

(*Chime.*)

fifty.

(ZOOT *begins to play a Christmas carol softly on the celeste while* CLIFTON *speaks.*)

You know, folks, this program is being transcribed for a broadcast abroad next month for some very special fellas overseas. And fellas, every week, we and hundreds of shows just like ours, get mail from you guys and we try to do our best to give you anything you want. Here's one of the Cavalcade's four-letter stars, with letters from the Army, the Navy, the Marine Corps and the Coast Guard. Miss Ann Collier.

[MUSIC NO. 22 "HAVE YOURSELF A MERRY LITTLE CHRISTMAS"]

(*"Applause" signs flash.* ANN *has just finished straightening* JOHNNY'S *tie, as he sits slumped in the chair. The Band starts playing "HAVE YOURSELF A MERRY LITTLE CHRISTMAS." She speaks over it.* LOU *stands next to her. His hat off. And he takes each letter from her as she finishes reading it. The lights Onstage are soft and nostalgic. Everyone is drifting in the thoughts that* ANN *brings up. Couples.* GINGER *finds* LOU. CLIFTON *is looking around the studio.* POPS *is standing and looking at the Christmas tree and adjusts the lights and cards.*)

ANN. Love to Nicholas in Hawaii from your mom and dad in Waban, Massachusetts. And to Dan Barley and the Radio Girls in Argentia, Newfoundland. And Yuletide greetings to the southern gentleman on Guadalcanal. Private Kenneally, in Australia, you're doing just fine, and love from Sara. And I've brought *all* of you a little gift, tied with the heart-strings of that girl back home.

(ANN *sings "MERRY LITTLE CHRISTMAS" and while she
does,* GENEVA *watches* ZOOT *play the piano. She puts her
hand on his shoulder. She sits down and plays the piano
with him.* LOU *and* GINGER *sit together next to the piano.*
LOU *looks at one of the letters which* ANN *read.* NEAL *is
looking out the door at some people walking outside the
studio.* B.J. *looks out the window, and drinks a cup of coffee.*)

CHRISTMAS FUTURE IS FAR AWAY
CHRISTMAS PAST IS PAST
CHRISTMAS PRESENT IS HERE TODAY
BRINGING JOY THAT WILL LAST
HAVE YOURSELF A MERRY LITTLE CHRISTMAS
LET YOUR HEART BE LIGHT
NEXT YEAR ALL OUR TROUBLES WILL BE OUT OF SIGHT
HAVE YOURSELF A MERRY LITTLE CHRISTMAS
MAKE THE YULETIDE GAY
NEXT YEAR ALL OUR TROUBLES WILL BE MILES AWAY
HERE WE ARE, AS IN OLDEN DAYS
HAPPY GOLDEN DAYS OF YORE
FAITHFUL FRIENDS WHO ARE DEAR TO US
GATHER NEAR TO US ONCE MORE
SOMEDAY SOON WE ALL WILL BE TOGETHER
IF THE FATES ALLOW
UNTIL THEN WE'LL HAVE TO MUDDLE THROUGH
    SOMEHOW
AND HAVE YOURSELF A MERRY LITTLE CHRISTMAS
    NOW

(*Band break. Then.*)
HAVE YOURSELF A MERRY LITTLE CHRISTMAS . . .
NOW.
(*"Applause" signs flash. They sing "STRIKE UP THE
BAND."*)

[MUSIC NO. 23 "STRIKE UP THE BAND"]
FULL COMPANY.
WE FOUGHT IN NINETEEN SEVENTEEN
RUM TA TA TUM TUM TUM
AND DROVE THE TYRANT FROM THE SCENE
RUM TA TA TUM TUM TUM

WE DIDN'T WANT ANOTHER WAR
BUT NOW WE'VE BEEN FORCED INTO ONE
THE FLAG THAT WE ARE FIGHTING FOR
IS THE RED AND WHITE AND BLUE ONE
WE DO NOT FAVOR WAR ALARMS
RUM TA TA TUM TUM TUM
BUT IF WE HEAR THE CALL TO ARMS
RUM TA TA TUM TUM
RUM TA TA TUM TUM
RUM TA TA TUM TUM TUM
LET THE DRUMS ROLL OUT
LET THE TRUMPET CALL
WHILE THE PEOPLE SHOUT
STRIKE UP THE BAND
HEAR THE CYMBALS RING
CALLING ONE AND ALL
TO THE MARTIAL SWING
STRIKE UP THE BAND

WOMEN.	MEN.
THERE IS WORK TO BE DONE, TO BE DONE	THERE IS WORK TO BE DONE
THERE'S A WAR TO BE WON, TO BE WON	THERE'S A WAR TO BE WON

ALL.
COME YOU SON OF A SON OF A GUN
TAKE YOUR STAND
FALL IN LINE YEA BO'
COME ALONG, LET'S GO
HEAY, LEADER, STRIKE UP THE BAND

(*Tap break.* CONNIE *in a spangled costume taps on a tap board brought out by* LOU, *who holds the center mic down close to it.*)

WITH OUR FLAG UNFURLED
FOR A BRAVE NEW WORLD
HEY, LEADER, STRIKE UP THE BAND

(*"Applause" signs flash.* STANLEY *lowers a tacky mirror ball on a rope. Music into "I'LL BE SEEING YOU."*)

[MUSIC NO. 24 "I'LL BE SEEING YOU"]

I'LL BE SEEING YOU IN ALL THE OLD FAMILIAR
   PLACES
THAT THIS HEART OF MINE EMBRACES ALL DAY
   THROUGH

(Band and dialog break. Then Company hums under:)

CLIFTON. Well, folks, that's our show for tonight. Dedicated
to the boys on the front. We'd like to stick around a little longer,
but we all have places to go, people to see, things to do. But we'll
be together when that little red light on your radio turns a deep
amber. Until next week, drive carefully and make that one for
the road a cup of coffee.

(Last chance.)

A cup of Maxwell House coffee, that perfect blend of java that's
toasted thousands for generations, good to the last drop. And so
this is Clifton Feddington, and the whole gang down at WOV
wishing you and yours the happiest and healthiest of holiday
cheer.

ANN. *(Singing.)*
I'LL FIND YOU IN THE MORNING SUN
   GROUP. *(Singing.)*
AND WHEN THE NIGHT IS NEW . . .
   JOHNNY. *(Pulling the mic over to him. Singing.)*
I'LL BE LOOKING AT THE MOON,
   GROUP. *(Singing quietly.* CLIFTON *conducts.)*
BUT I'LL BE SEEING YOU.
   CLIFTON. Bye bye. *(Band chord.)* And buy bonds.

[MUSIC NO. 25 "MUTUAL MANHATTAN VARIETY CAVALCADE"]

(Band chord. CLIFTON *conducts the last note and the lights blip
   out, leaving only the studio practicals.* LOU *checks his stop
   watch. And records the time. The Band plays the
   "MUTUAL MANHATTAN VARIETY CAVALCADE"
   theme song while the Cast dash around, getting coats,
   straightening up, etc. They go off the air* before *the last
   note is played. (the last note is never played.)* STANLEY
   *speaks from the booth, lights switch to studio lighting and
   the audience, as far as the Characters are concerned, have
   left.)*

STANLEY. That's it, we're off the air.

(*Everyone bustles around, getting coats, chatting.* CLIFTON *speaks over them.*)

CLIFTON. Thank you everyone.

(CANTONE *has gone to the piano and sits down.* LOU *is cleaning up.*)

LOU. That's it everybody.
CLIFTON. Thank you everyone, that was a swell show.
LOU. Nice show everybody! (*He bustles around already to get everything finished so he can leave.*) Gimme a hand, Stanley.
                    (STANLEY *does. All a chattering.*)
CLIFTON. Call tomorrow at nine.
GENEVA. Nine!
                    (*Musicians grumble.*)
CLIFTON. Orchestra at two.
                    (*Musicians cheer.*)
Now we're only paid-up until ten thirty so get your wraps and leave quickly.
                    (*Clock says 10:20.*)
LOU. Shouters at nine, plumbers at two! Move it!
CLIFTON. I'd like to see B.J. In my office at half-past eight.
LOU. (*From wherever he's working.*) B.J., eight-thirty.
CLIFTON. Neal, 8:45.
LOU. Neal, quarter 'til.
NEAL. What'd I do?
CLIFTON. And Geneva, can you come in a few minutes before rehearsal?
GENEVA. Child, I can't make it till noon.
CLIFTON. Geneva, do me a favor, would you? . . .
GENEVA. (*Heading Off down the hall,* CLIFTON *after her.*) Honey we're gonna be playing tonight till after two and if you think . . .
NEAL. Did I do something wrong?
LOU. Musicians, you will use the 44th Street Exit please. You can pick up your pay envelopes downstairs, and please musicians, do not drop the empty pay envelopes in the stairwell. Also no paper cups and no instruments left lying around where they are not supposed to be. The paper cups go in receptacles, the instruments in your lockers. And do not put out your cigarettes on the floors. Use an ashtray . . . oh.

(*No Musicians left.* WALLY *is sitting alone in the only chair that's left.* POPS *is cleaning a few mugs and hanging them back up on the pegs on the wall. Then he straightens his desk. Carefully folds the newspaper he has been reading and puts it in the lowest drawer.*)

CLIFTON. (*Re-entering with pay envelopes.*) Okay, everyone, here's your pay. I'm giving the envelopes to Lou to hand out.

(*Everyone moves to the pay.* LOU *calls out names. Ad-libbed responses. Some find five dollar bonuses, some don't.*)

LOU. (*Quietly.*) Miss Brooks. Mr. Tilden. Miss Miller. Miss Collier. Mr. Baker—excuse me, Second Lt. Baker. Mr. Gibson, Miss Browne, Mr. Doubleman, Mr. Cohn.

CLIFTON. (*To* WALLY *who is alone.*) Wally, thanks a lot. That was very good. You did fine. (*Giving him a dollar bill from his wallet.*) Here. No, you deserve it.

GINGER. That's you, Lou.

WALLY. Mr. Feddington? I can come in early tomorrow if you like.

CLIFTON. That won't be necessary, Wally. Thank you.

WALLY. I'll be around. You don't have to pay me.

CLIFTON. It was a swell show, really it was. And you can come by any time you like. Hey, looks like you've got some deliveries to make.

B.J. Okay, Neal, where are we going?

BIFF. Doesn't look like anybody's going too far.

GINGER. It's like the North Pole out there.

B.J. Okay, Neal, where are we going?

CONNIE. Ginger, let's go make snow angels.

            (CONNIE *and* GINGER *exit into the alley.*)

NEAL. How about the Horn and Hardart?

B.J. The what?

                    (BIFF *laughs.*)

GINGER. Let's go to Sardi's.

B.J. That's a great idea . . . Sardi's. (B.J. *goes Off Right to get his coat.*)

NEAL. (*Not such a great idea. Worried about money.*) Sardi's?

BIFF. Sardi's is fine.

GENEVA. Come on, Biff, Zoot and I are taking you to the Onyx Club.

NEAL. I can't get in there.

BIFF. Who's playing?

ZOOT. We are.

ANN. Come on, Biff, we want to show you off.

BIFF. Okay. You go ahead. I'll meet you there.

ZOOT. How're you getting there?

BIFF. (*Going Off Right to get his coat.*) Walk. Ten blocks.

ZOOT. (*To* NEAL *who is sitting on the step at the Downstage edge of the greenroom.*) Hey, Neal, for someone who saw that arrangement for the first time, you did pretty good. (ZOOT *exits to the alley.*)

NEAL. (*Following* ZOOT *out.*) Hey, Zoot, can I buy you a drink?
        (CONNIE *re-enters with snow all over her coat.*)

CONNIE. (*Calling Off Right.*) B.J., come on.

B.J. (*Entering in coat and galoshes.*) Just a second.

(*Crosses across the now dark studio except for the ghost light to speak to* CLIFTON *who is locking his office door.*)

CLIFTON. Well, another one down.

B.J. Mr. Feddington, I just want to thank you.

CLIFTON. Thank *you*, B.J.

B.J. This is a great opportunity for me.

CLIFTON. We'll talk tomorrow.

B.J. I did well, didn't I?

CLIFTON. You did fine. We'll talk tomorrow.

B.J. (*A little disappointed.*) Well. Good night.

CLIFTON. Night, B.J.

CONNIE. (*As they leave.*) Night, Popsy.

B.J. Night, Pops. (*They are gone.*)

LOU. (*Crossing to* CLIFTON.) Well, I'm about done it looks like, Clifton.

CLIFTON. (*Real cheery.*) Thank you, Lou.

LOU. Good show tonight.

CLIFTON. It was a good show tonight.

LOU. (*Shyly.*) Thanks for the bonus.

CLIFTON. Sure. Hey, why don't you stick around for me and we'll go get a cup of coffee. I'll only be a minute or two.

GINGER. (*Re-entering.*) Lou?

LOU. Ahhh. I gotta . . . get home. If you know what I mean.

(GINGER *is tapping her foot mouthing "Come on" to* LOU. CLIFTON *catches on.*)

CLIFTON. Oh. Sure. Right. Well, see you tomorrow then.

LOU. Right. See you tomorrow, Clifton. Night Biff. Good luck.

GINGER. Come on, everybody'll be gone by the time we get there.

STANLEY. Merry Christmas, Ginger.

GINGER. Merry Christmas. Lou, come on!

LOU. Keep your pants on. I'm an executive around here.

(LOU *and* GINGER *exit.* BIFF *enters.*)

CLIFTON. Biff.

BIFF. Cliff-tone. (*They both laugh softly.*)

CLIFTON. Hey, don't forget your horn.

BIFF. Keep it for me, Clifton.

(*A pause.* JOHNNY *stares straight ahead.* CLIFTON *looks at* BIFF. POPS *at his desk shakes his head.* WALLY *is puzzled by it all.* WALLY *looks around.* JOHNNY *looks down at the piano keys.* POPS *down at his desk.* BIFF *steps to the door and opens it.* POPS *looks at* BIFF.)

I'll pick it up after the War.

(BIFF *salutes.* WALLY *unconsciously salutes back.* BIFF *leaves. No one moves.* WALLY *looks around.* POPS *is looking at a picture he has on his desk.*)

WALLY. (*Quietly.*) I'm gonna sign up. (WALLY *exits.*)

CLIFTON. (*After a beat.*) Well, Johnny. Good luck . . . I . . . well, see you tomorrow, Johnny. Don't be late.

(CLIFTON *starts out. Stops at* POPS' *desk to adjust his muffler.* POPS *extends his hand palm up.*)

Oh, Pops, I almost forgot. (*Gets out a dollar bill to give him.*) Thank you very much.

(POPS *looks at it and leaves his hand out.*)

Right. Thank you, Pops. (CLIFTON *pulls his muffler tighter and his knit cap or hat with flaps further down over his head.*) Now don't stay here all night, okay, Pops? Saul wants us out of the building—

POPS. What do you think, I live here?

(CLIFTON *leaves.* JOHNNY *gets up and puts on his coat and hat and walks to the door.*)

JOHNNY. (*As he leaves.*) Don't wait up for me.

POPS. (*Preoccupied.*) Mm.

(JOHNNY *turns and goes in the opposite direction as everyone else when he gets outside.* POPS *goes to the door. It's still snowing. He pulls his sweater up around his neck. You can hear the folks playing in the snow outside. Dialogue and*

*laughter. Snowball fight. Some sing "DECK THE
HALLS" from the radio drama.*)

NEAL. (*Off.*) Hey cut that out.
B.J. (*Off.*) Hey, Cliff, that's a great hat.
CONNIE. (*Off.*) Don't B.J. don't. That's cold.
           (*Screams. Laughter.*)
NEAL. (*Off.*) Will somebody help me dig out my cab?
GINGER. (*Off.*) Come on, Clifton, don't be such a poop.
STANLEY. (*Off.*) Hey, Mr. Cohn, can I come too?
LOU. (*Off.*) Night, Mr. Feddington.

(POPS *listens and the sounds fade away. He shuts the door and
turns off most of the lights in the room. The studio is lit only by the ghost light and all is as it was at the beginning.* ANN
comes in quietly from the outside as POPS *stands surveying
the studio proudly.*)

ANN. Pops, I almost forgot. I wanted to give you something.
Merry Christmas, Pops. (*She presents him with a gift; a long
thin box. He takes it and holds it in both hands without
moving.*)
POPS. (*Softly.*) Thank you. (*She kisses him.*) Thank you.

(*She leaves as quietly as she came in. He looks at the present and
starts to open it, but changes his mind and puts it under his
tree. He turns on his desk radio. While it warms up, he
takes out a glass, a toothbrush, which he puts into the glass,
and a towel. Static from the radio. He tunes through several
stations. Cities from all over the country. We hear occasional words indentifying something or other like "WEAF
Swing Shift" and "blizzard conditions existing for most of
the Northeast tonight," dance bands and their announcers,
the end of a War update, or other news, finally to music.
The Claude Thornhill theme: "Snowfall."* POPS *picks up
his towel and glass and toothbrush and walks Off toward
the left hall. When he gets into the studio, he does a simple
little softshoe step in the light spill on the floor, laughs
twice, then goes Off down the hall. Lights fade to black.*)

APPENDIX A

Sound Effects

For the sound effects, there is an effects table on which is a performing space, partially carpeted, partially bare wood. Around that space are the various effects. On either end of the table are the larger effects: at the left end on and above the table level is the window and curtain effect which is nothing more than a half-size window with weights inside the window frame. The curtain effect is simply curtain rings on a curtain rod, joined together with string since there is no curtain, with a dowel connected to the most upstage ring with which the curtain rings are drawn, thus making the sound. Below the window and under the effects table is a wind machine: a drum with wood slats lengthwise which is free to turn by a crank and a piece of thick canvas positioned over the drum so that when it is cranked, the wood slats rub against the canvas and cause the wind sound to be produced. On the right end of the table from the floor level to about a foot above the table is a half-size door unit, complete with hardware and locks. The various other effects are positioned around these larger effects at the most convenient places for LOU to reach them.

The table should be heavily miked: under the working space, the wind machine and a "wand" mic which is nothing more than a mic attached to the top part of a boom mic stand. This "wand" mic can be held by LOU to get closer to the effect he might be doing. There should probably be a boom mic hanging over the table, which, if it is period, completes the image and gives the whole table a little more liveness.

(Note: the Sound Effects Man is very much an actor as he "performs" the effects. He should be encouraged to "perform" these effects with as much ham as possible.)

Pepsi Cola
(Performed at the effects table)
   1. ice cubes: two large nuts or bolts dropped into a drinking glass.
   2. the "quish" sound: vocal effect.
   3. pouring liquid: water into the glass.
   4. fizz: drop some Alka Seltzer into the water.

Comedy Routine
(Performed at the effects table)

85

    1. door slam: the door unit.

    2. telephone ringing: a practical telephone with receiver.

How About You (Softshoe routine)

(Performed at the left mic on little waist high platform brought over to the mic)

    1. Sand paper on 2x4 wood blocks and shoes, corresponding to the choreography the two kids do.

Mysterious Curtains

(Performed at the effects table wheeled to just left of center)

1. sleigh bells: actual sleigh bells.
2. dog barks: vocal sound done into a drinking glass.
3. carriage on cobblestones: a special effect which is free-standing and not part of the effects table made with wheels which turn by a crank and roll over loose slate. (optional)
4. hooves: coconut halves on the working space.
5. door locks: on the door unit.
6. striking of beggar: one hand slapping the other.
7. falling down: forearms on carpeted area of working space.
8. snow walking: squeezing a box of cornstarch.
9. plunger wind: a plumber's helper stuck into the pants so that the plunger is mouth height. Blow into it while "walking in the snow."
10. door: actual sound.
11. hand warming: actual sound.
12. climbing stairs: shoes on hands. Toes of each on uncarpeted part of work space.
13. keys: actual sound.
14. window breaking: a special effect. Can be the lower part of the carriage effects box. A handle on a hinge with a screw protruding from the under side which, when dropped on a slim plate of glass, breaks it and sends the pieces falling below into a receptacle full of other pieces of glass and metal strips. (optional)
15. pillow: actual sound.
16. covers (bed clothes): flipping a piece of cloth.
17. chimes: a child's xylophone.
18. ticking: a large wind-up alarm clock miked very closely.
19. breaking down door: crushing a berry box close to the mic.

Nash

(Performed at the effects table still in its *Mysterious Curtains* position)

1. troops marching: a foot square unit. Wood frame, within which are suspended dozens of wooden pegs from strings. When held above the wooden, uncarpeted part of the work space and dropped in marching tempo, each peg touches at a slightly different time and it sounds like marching soldiers.

(Note: there is no reason why more effects cannot be used or different ones substituted for the ones listed. There are many books on the subject, most of them printed in the fifties. The most useful was one called *Sound Effects Today* which included an encyclopedia-like listing of effects and complete construction diagrams.)

APPENDIX B

Copy for "fake" program

CLIFTON A. FEDDINGTON, with his partner, Saul Lebowitz, has been producing *The Mutual Manhattan Variety Cavalcade* since its inception six years ago last week. It's been a long climb for Clifton and his *Cavalcade*. He began at WHK in Cleveland in the much-acclaimed children's program, *Let's have lunch with Mr. Cliff*. Then, on to Philadelphia where local radio audiences tuned in nightly to a community radio theatre group, *The Feddington Players*. Then, in 1935, with seed money from sixteen sponsors, Mr. Feddington landed a fifteen-minute musical variety show called *Stars in Heaven* which featured his recent singing discoveries, Ann Collier and Johnny Cantone, the Zoot Doubleman Quartet and Neal Tilden. In 1936, Mutual expanded the show to a half-hour and re-named it *The Mutual Half-Hour of Singing Stars* and the team added its first Gibson brother, Bobby. Just last January, through a deal with New York's *WOV* Radio, the show became the hour-long *Cavalcade* we love today and tonight's show is the last in our first season. Mr. Feddington also is President of *Clifton Records* (the signature series), which will be into production as soon as the ASCAP strike is settled.

JOHNNY CANTONE first excited listeners in his native Brooklyn, New York where Johnny opened the '39 Pro-Am Duckpin Tourney with his version of The Star Spangled Banner. Since then he has sung "The Anthem" at hundreds of sporting events (including his own unsuccessful attempt to unseat the defending welter-weight champ Eldon Dwight). Now "featured vocalist" with *WOV's Cavalcade,* Johnny has come a long way from those clubs in Jersey where he fronted bands for five years before the Cavalcade happened along. "The Tone" hopes to begin his acting career with his upcoming engagement to read Odets with Harold on Don McNeill's *Breakfast Club* in March. He also hopes to be able to spend more time with his wife, Angel. Soon.

GINGER BROOKS moved everything to New York in the fall of 1940. It was only a year until she landed the coveted position of microphone monitor at WACL. But it wasn't long before she was cutting records for Artie Shaw. But her real forte was singing so she left the technical position and became an overnight success as the only singing waitress and stacker at *Romeo's Spaghetti House,* where our stage manager and choreographer, Lou Cohn, discovered her. Ginger's favorite color is red.

GENEVA LEE BROWNE began her show business career at the Cotton Club in *The Hot Chocolates Revue,* and later, with Earl "Fatha" Hines. In 1939, she moved to Kansas City where she formed her own jazz quintet, The Kansas City Browne Boys, and, until this fall, entertained listeners there nightly at the Chesterfield Club. Since September, she has recorded for *Victor, Okey,* and *Vocalion* Records and has just signed a contract to sing with Jimmy Lunceford's Orchestra. She has also been offered a film short with Louis Armstrong and Ethel Waters to be shot at The Cotton Club where she began singing six years ago which will feature a song she has written and performed as part of her set with her group nightly at the Onyx Club.

ANN COLLIER was singing with her sisters in Montclair, New Jersey when she was only seven. When she went away to school, she worked on WJSV's Dr. Pepper Parade on Sunday nights and was offered tours with Claude Thornhill and the King Biscuit Entertainers. In '35, she returned to her native Montclair and sang with dance bands there where she was discovered by *WOV's* own Clifton Feddington and swept into New York and into the limelight of his *Cavalcade* where she was "featured vocalist" for three years. She has been with the show for six years now and we hope she'll be here for six more. Ann lives with her four year old son Matthew on the Upper East Side of Manhattan.

ZOOT DOUBLEMAN comes to *WOV* fresh from a USO tour of training bases in sunny California, a duty he reluctantly performs in lieu of military service. A founding member of The Chuck Cabot Orchestra, Zoot owes his entire musical career to the genius of Mrs. Pearl Fishman. He has played sessions with such well-known bands as Art Lathan's Bearcats, Irv Fein's Fabulous Three and Murray O'Toole's Rover Boys. A serious musician at heart (he attended Brooklyn College), his new composition, *Zoot Suite,* is scheduled for performance in the near future at Carnegie Hall or in Pittsburgh.

B.J. GIBSON is the youngest of the singing Gibson brothers, who began their musical careers in New Orleans in 1932 (B.J. was fourteen) in an act their father named *Three Boys and a Harmonica.* With his brothers "over there," B.J. packed Bobby's harmonica, Buddy's sweater, and his father's arrangements and went up to New Haven where he is a Senior English major at Yale's Branford College. He comes into New York every week though to do the show, keeping up the Gibson tradition, and is now singin' and dancin' and smilin' his way into the hearts of radio listeners everywhere. "Welcome aboard, B.J."

CONNIE MILLER comes all the way from Ogden, Utah where she studied tap, ballet, and ballroom at Madame Stephen's Dance Academy. At age ten, she and her mother lived in Los Angeles and while she was working as a script girl for Columbia Pictures she kept the crews entertained with her imitations of Shirley Temple and Margaret O'Brien. After not being cast as Robert Young's daughter in *Joe Smith, American,* Connie and her mom came to New York and auditioned for Clifton at *WOV.* Now the youngest member of the *Cavalcade,* Connie hopes one day to become a Rockette.

RAY OWEN has a long career of seemingly endless talents. From the critically acclaimed "third quizmaster" on KFJ's *Questions, Please,* to the corny magician of WBAL's *Vaudeville at Noon.* And who can forget WTAM's *Live from Cleveland?* Ray also co-starred with Nigel Nooley in the RKO short *Shelby's Millions.* But possibly Ray's greatest gift is his interpretation of "the ballad' and it is there that Ray becomes an indispensable member of the *Cavalcade.*

NEAL TILDEN's career with some of the greats and many of the near-greats is pretty much history now. The grueling singing lessons, the one-night stands, until he exploded on the vocal horizon with Nestor Nugent's Tornadoes at Tarrytown's Cafe O'Ola. On to greater heights, and the fabled nine-week tour of '34 with the late, great Wes Westerley, who after losing Neal, lamented, "It was like losing a horn." Neal has been with the *Cavalcade* since before it was even a twinkle in Clifton's eye, and he still keeps a hand in club singing, and a hand in radio singing, and a hand in stage acting too (he was recently up for the role of the understudy to Gil Strutton, Jr. in the Broadway smash *Best Foot Forward*). But his first love is the *Cavalcade,* and he says he's delighted to be handling vocal chores with and "O.K. outfit" like ours "Thanks, Neal!"

WOV Radio, 1280 kc, 730 Fifth Avenue, New York, Circle 5-7979

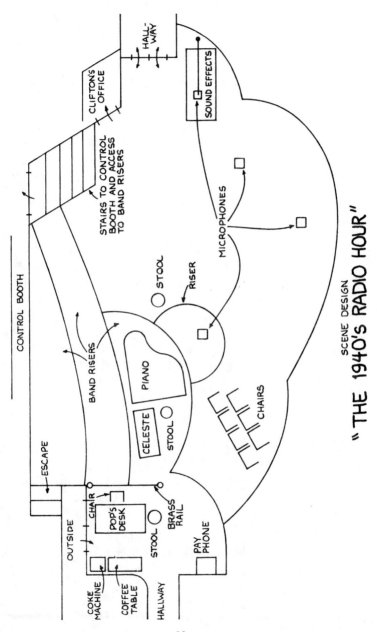

SCENE DESIGN
"THE 1940's RADIO HOUR"

CONTROL BOOTH

CLIFTON'S OFFICE

HALL-WAY

SOUND EFFECTS

STAIRS TO CONTROL
BOOTH AND ACCESS
TO BAND RISERS

MICROPHONES

STOOL

RISER

BAND RISERS

ESCAPE

PIANO

CELESTE

STOOL

CHAIRS

OUTSIDE

CHAIR

POP'S DESK

STOOL

BRASS RAIL

PAY PHONE

HALLWAY

COKE MACHINE

COFFEE TABLE

93

THE MUSICAL OF MUSICALS (THE MUSICAL!)
Music by Eric Rockwell
Lyrics by Joanne Bogart
Book by Eric Rockwell and Joanne Bogart

2m, 2f / Musical / Unit Set

The Musical of Musicals (The Musical!) is a musical about musicals! In this hilarious satire of musical theatre, one story becomes five delightful musicals, each written in the distinctive style of a different master of the form, from Rodgers and Hammerstein to Stephen Sondheim. The basic plot: June is an ingenue who can't pay the rent and is threatened by her evil landlord. Will the handsome leading man come to the rescue? The variations are: a Rodgers & Hammerstein version, set in Kansas in August, complete with a dream ballet; a Sondheim version, featuring the landlord as a tortured artistic genius who slashes the throats of his tenants in revenge for not appreciating his work; a Jerry Herman version, as a splashy star vehicle; an Andrew Lloyd Webber version, a rock musical with themes borrowed from Puccini; and a Kander & Ebb version, set in a speakeasy in Chicago. This comic valentine to musical theatre was the longest running show in the York Theatre Company's 35-year history before moving to Off-Broadway.